Feather: Swan Maidens Retold

DEMELZA CARLTON

A tale in the Romance a Medieval Fairy Tale series

One

"If we don't do it naked, we disrespect the old deities," Swanhild declared, pulling off her shift.

Raphael glanced around, then reluctantly removed his tunic. "That may be, but if Father Fazzio finds us, like he did the others, the whole town will hear of it, and we'll be listening to interminable sermons about chastity and purity for the next month." As his eyes rested on Swanhild's, the lust heating them said a month's worth of sermons was a small price to pay.

"Father Fazzio is afraid of the old pagan groves. He would never venture so far into the forest, and even if he did, the old gods would hide us from his sight, if we worship them properly."

Raphael lay down on the grass, and stretched his hands out in supplication. "It is you I wish to worship, not some god, old or new. Come here."

Swanhild laughed, stretching her arms above her head to better show off her breasts, before she perched herself astride Raphael's hips. He was ready for her, as always, but she took pleasure in teasing him, rubbing herself against him, until he could take it no more.

Today, he seemed to be feasting his eyes on her breasts, as she worked her way to a climax. It came fast today, and she arched her back as she cried out to the forest canopy above.

Raphael was rock hard beneath her, but still

he didn't enter her.

"You're so beautiful," he breathed, reaching up to cup her breasts. "Marry me, Swanhild."

"No," she said, grinding against him again. She closed her eyes, pressing down harder. Surely she couldn't be about to climax again. Oh, but she was. She cried out for joy.

"Marry me, so that we may do this every day and every night," he said, staring up at her adoringly.

Swanhild laughed. "How is that different to what we do now? Come, Raphael, I am about to climax for the third time, and I am doing all the work!"

"The forest floor is fine in summer," he said, caressing her breasts. "But when the autumn rains come…or the cold winter snow, I want to be warm…inside…" Finally, he thrust into her, timing it perfectly to send her over the edge of another climax. "With you, in our bed. I want you to be my wife, Swanhild."

Something about the angle he'd chosen sent waves of pleasure through her, building to another, impossible peak.

"I care nothing for autumn, or winter. What I want is you, her and now, in this moment, just as we are…now!" For the first time, they'd timed it perfectly, reaching their peak together. With more practice, they might manage this every time.

She cried out his name, but his shout sounded more like, "Marry me, Swanhild!"

She shook her head as they broke apart, and headed to the small spring that inevitably graced these holy groves so that she might wash.

Wash, dry, dress – it was a ritual of its own, one she'd completed three times today, twice in this grove. But they would have to leave soon, to make it home before dark, and any more lovemaking would have to wait until tomorrow.

She hoped he'd come up with a more acceptable marriage proposal before autumn, instead of his heat of the moment demands that would mean nothing when they were clothed once more. At least, to most men they meant nothing, or so her mother had said. Promises made in passion were worthless – and her mother would know, for her father had often promised never to beat her again, only to do so the next day.

But Raphael was nothing like her father, she reminded herself, as his gentle healer's hand closed around hers. One day he would choose the right moment, and she would see his eyes light up when she said…

They'd reached the edge of the forest, and Raphael had dropped to his knees, setting his basket down. He placed hers beside it, so that he might take both of her hands in his.

"Swanhild, I love you more than the sun in the sky, or the life-giving air that lets us draw breath. I love your body, I love your mind, I love your magic, and I love the sound of your voice. I would give my life to spend whatever moments I might have left with you. I know a witch and an apprentice apothecary are an unlikely match, for while we are apart, we compete for the same customers every day, but when we are together…ah, we are so much more. You are my dearest friend, my only love, and I beg you to become my wife. Please, Swanhild, whether it is today or tomorrow or next year, or a hundred years from now, promise you will marry me, because I love no one else, and I never will."

She stared into his eyes. This was the moment.

"Yes," she breathed.

Raphael's mouth dropped open. "What did you say?"

Swanhild laughed. "I said yes. My dress is ready, and we only need to tell my mother, before we may set a date. You'd better make good on your promise to make love to me morning and night, though, or I shall have to take you out into the forest and leave you for the old gods to deal with!"

He rose to his feet and wrapped his arms around her. "Whatever you desire. With you as my wife, I will give you anything you desire."

She laughed. "Then you may start now, with a kiss."

One kiss turned into several, and the sun had set by the time they emerged from the trees, hand in hand. But the darkness didn't bother them, for what could possibly mar such perfect joy?

Two

"Where have you been? I feared the worst!" Mother seized Swanhild's shoulders and stared at her. "Are you feverish? Have you started to cough? Any painful swellings?"

Swanhild had been a witch long enough to know what those symptoms meant. Her mother thought she was late home because she'd caught the plague. "I'm fine!" she snapped, trying to pull out of her mother's grasp, but she wouldn't be shaken.

"Good, good," Mother said vaguely, staring out into the night. She shook herself. "Then we must keep you that way. There is not a moment to lose!"

She dragged Swanhild out the door and down the road, until her boots splashed into the lake. Cold water washed over the top of them, swirling around her toes and threatening to slip off her shoes. She mustn't have fastened them properly, for it seemed her feet were swimming in shoes that had fitted fine in the forest.

And why was Mother suddenly growing taller?

Water seeped through her sleeves. Swanhild flung her arms up, out of the water, but they didn't feel right. Lighter, somehow. And she could see both arms at the same time, one on either side, filling her sleeves…no, slipping out of her sleeves…

Realisation hit her like a punch to the gut. "Mother! Why are you using magic on me?" she cried.

"It's the only way to save you. All the swans in the kingdom are protected by the Queen, so you shall be safe from hunters, too."

"What do you mean…what are you protecting me from?" Swanhild tried to say, but only a horrible honking sound came out. Like a swan protecting her nest. "Mother!"

"Fly, fly away. When the plague is gone and it is safe to return, then you may resume your true form. Stand upon this shore, and if it is safe, you shall transform. But not before. Begone!" Mother flapped her arms, as if to shoo Swanhild away, deeper into the lake.

Some primal fear seized Swanhild's innards, and she found herself flapping, too. Wheeling around, lifting, gliding…her feet left the water and she flew across the surface of the lake, fleeing from her home and everything she'd ever known.

She wanted to turn, to head back, but the instinct to fly from danger was too strong.

One day, she would come back. Conquer and command this silly swan form to take her home. For it would be safe to return, she was certain of it.

12

Three

Raphael knew he should go home. He should tell his master, Gojko the apothecary, that he wanted to get married, and ask if he might end his apprenticeship early so that he might start earning enough to support a family. Well, just a wife at first, but the amount of time he spent naked with Swanhild, a family wouldn't be far off.

Instead, he lingered outside Swanhild's house. Gojko would not be pleased if he went inside the witch's house, for that is what the master called Swanhild's mother, Tola. On anyone else's lips, the word would not have sounded so sour, for even Tola herself was happy to claim the title of being the town witch, but when Gojko said it, it was with the same venom he reserved for demons, fleas and rats.

Hence he wanted to be certain Gojko would approve the end of his apprenticeship before confessing that he planned to marry Tola's daughter. Perhaps the man would be more accepting of the two women if he knew that both possessed real magic, as well as knowing as much about healing and herbs as Gojko himself, but Raphael doubted it. Gojko was a bitter old man who liked to hold a grudge, and Tola had once saved someone's life when Gojko had given up treating them, convinced no potion could possibly work when all he knew had failed.

So Tola became that foreign witch who did deals with the devil, at least in Gojko's house, and Raphael was not allowed to speak of her.

Yet here she was, bursting out the door of her own home, dragging Swanhild behind her as she hurried down to the lake.

So Tola hadn't liked the idea of Swanhild marrying him. For what else could anger the woman so, except today's news?

Raphael stepped into the shadows, so Tola wouldn't see him, before following the pair. There was no way he'd allow his future wife to face her mother's magical wrath alone.

Tola dragged Swanhild to the very edge of the lake, then pushed her in. Swanhild stumbled forward at her mother's push, but she didn't lose her footing in the knee-deep waters.

Light glinted off a blade in Tola's hand.

Raphael opened his mouth to cry out a warning to Swanhild, then almost choked as Tola turned the blade on herself, slashing it across her arm before shifting the blade to the other hand and slicing her other arm, too. The knife tumbled from her fingers into the sand at her feet, and Raphael found he could breathe again. Tola meant to cast a spell, not stab her daughter.

Only then did Swanhild turn to face her mother, her feet still in the lake. She crouched down, staring up at Tola with a look of horror on her face.

Her arms stretched out, splashing the surface of the water as if trying to drive it away.

And then…she changed.

Arms became wings, and her gown slipped off faster than it had when they'd made love in the forest.

"Mother! Why are you using magic on me?" she cried.

For a moment, Raphael saw the woman he loved, crouching in the water, wings outspread, and then she was gone. A swan sat there in her place, flapping her wings and honking like she was trying to drive away a predator from her nest.

Horror froze his tongue.

The swan who had been his betrothed wheeled around and took flight across the lake.

Despair freed it.

"Mistress Tola, how could you do such a thing to your own daughter?"

Tola started to turn, then staggered around to face him. "I would do anything to save her."

Raphael saw red. "What in heaven's name would be so bad about her marrying me? I would support her and care for her and love her all the days of my life!"

"Can you cure the plague, boy?"

The plague? Like the one that wiped out Altino?

"Of course not. No one can," Raphael said. That was why Mistress Sara had insisted no strangers would be welcomed in their town. And no matter what Elder Ahab or Father Fazzio said, there wasn't a man, woman or child in Mirroten brave enough to disobey Mistress Sara.

Tola fell to her knees. Only now did Raphael see the dark rivulets of blood running down her arms. She'd sliced open her veins, he was sure of it.

He rushed forward. "Mistress Tola, you must let me help you, or you shall die!"

She held up a bloodied hand. "I must do no such thing, boy. If you have any sense, and you hope to live long enough to marry my daughter, you will stay as far away from me as you can. I nursed poor Ysabel until the plague killed her, but not before she passed the pestilence to me, her father and likely the priest, too. Death comes to us all, but I shall choose the time and the place, not some disease. I give my life for my daughter, so that she may live." She coughed, and brought up blood, spitting it on the ground, away from Raphael. "Tell Sara to run. Far and fast and to somewhere she can close the gates to everyone. Her family's fortress, high in the mountains, maybe. Tell her to wait as long as she can to return. A year. Maybe two. Until news reaches her that it is safe. Then, you may return here, and Swanhild…Swanhild…"

She tipped over on her side, her breathing laboured.

"Mistress Tola, if you would but wrap the sleeve tightly around your arm, it might slow the bleeding. You may yet live."

Tola began to laugh, which only made her cough. "Sara will need you with your unquenchable hope when she goes. You see she gets somewhere safe. When it is safe to return home, Swanhild will come here, and if you truly love her, you will be here waiting when she does. And my daughter…you see you make her happy, boy. For if you ever beat her, I'll send the devil himself to rip out your intestines and whip you to death with them."

"And I thought you'd come back as a ghost and turn me into a frog," Raphael said. Oh, he was a fool. He should have thought of it sooner. "No, wait. Turn me into a swan, like Swanhild. Then we'll both be safe together, and when we come back…"

"Not enough magic left in my blood to turn you into anything, boy. You'll have to take your chances with Sara and whoever else you can save. Now go! Get those long legs up to the church and light a candle for Ysabel, and anyone else whose soul might help carry your prayers to heaven. For you'll need all the luck in the world to survive this." Another cough, weaker this time. "Go or I might try to change you into a slug after all. I might have enough magic for that…"

Raphael swallowed. "And how will I be able to face Swanhild, when I see her again, if I let her mother die alone?"

Silence was his only answer. Not even the sound of Tola drawing one last breath, for she'd released hers already.

Her dying words, her last wish…had been for Swanhild. He had to survive, to bring word to Swanhild of her mother's last moments, her love for her daughter. And he had to make her happy.

"Yes, Mistress Tola, I swear on my own life, I will," Raphael said. He was reluctant to leave her there, but there was nothing he could do for her now. Father Fazzio was the one who delivered last rites, and saw to it that bodies were buried in the churchyard.

So he legged it up to the church, where he met Tobias at the door.

"Where have you been?" Tobias hissed. "I told Father Fazzio you were coming, that you would never miss Ysabel's vigil, but now he's gone up to see Gojko to get you! Quick, get inside, so we can tell him you arrived just after he left."

Inside the church, where he could light a candle for Ysabel, and Tola, and maybe a couple for his parents, too. Because if the plague had truly come to Mirroten, like Tola said, then she was right that every prayer counted.

Raphael nodded and led the way inside.

Four

Swanhild could think of nothing but the rush of wind beneath her wings, buoying her up and away to…ah, that was her destination. Instinct had her angling down, toward a bevy of swans sitting on the shore. No, sleeping on the shore.

This was a safe place to sleep.

She landed roughly, suddenly aware of how much her arms…no, her wings ached. But here she could rest, because the other swans knew it would be safe.

She should stay here, with them, until she could return home.

Yes.

She settled on the damp sand, tucking her head under her wing.

Here it was safe for a swan like her to sleep.

If she'd been herself, Swanhild might have worried about Raphael, or her mother, or what the future would hold. But a swan saw no further than the next meal, and there was waterweed aplenty in the shallows, so the swan who was once Swanhild slept, as serene as the mirror-like lake that gave Mirroten its name.

But Mirroten was anything but serene.

Five

At the end of the vigil, when people started to slip out of the church, Father Fazzio stayed standing in front of the altar. He coughed, then said, "All the young people of Mirroten, I ask but a moment of your time. Children and youths and even adults who are not yet married. Boys and girls alike. I ask you to go home, pack a bag for a week's travel, and return here, within the hour. I have a quest, a most holy quest, for all of you. You have been

chosen to go on a crusade to save Mirroten –
but you must make haste! Quickly, now. Go
and pack a bag, then bring it right back here!"

He shooed them out of the church, his eyes
fever-bright with the sort of madness Raphael
had only seen in those near to death. When the
priest coughed again, Raphael was sure of it –
Tola had been right. The man was infected by
the plague.

Raphael drifted out of the church, his mind
awash with worry. He didn't surface until
someone seized his arm and yanked, hard,
bringing him face to face with Silvana, the girl
whose father owned the mill. She did not look
pleased.

Raphael held his hands up in surrender.
"Whatever it is, it wasn't me!"

She made a disgusted sound. "Of course
not, you fool. I'd let you go with all the other
sheep if I thought this was your doing. Unless
you've given the priest some potion that drove
him to this madness?"

Raphael shook his head. "Never! Mistress

Tola said he's infected with the plague."

Silvana swore. She turned to Tobias. "Did you know this?"

Now it was Tobias's turn to shake his head. "No, this is the first I have heard of it. Where can he have caught it?"

"Mistress Tola said Ysabel had it first, and it spread to her father…and to Father Fazzio."

Silvana's brow furrowed further. "Does Mistress Sara know? Someone must tell her."

Raphael did not consider himself a coward, but he knew he did not have the courage to bring bad news to Mistress Sara. "Tobias? She's your mum…"

Silvana shook her head. "I shall tell her. You two, go get your things, and get back to the church. Do what you can to keep the others away from Father Fazzio and his foolish crusade." She stabbed a finger at Raphael, "They will listen to you because you're the apprentice healer, and they'll listen to Tobias because he's Sara's son. Don't let him send anyone anywhere."

Raphael found himself nodding in agreement. Logically, he knew Silvana was younger than him, and he had no need to follow any order she gave, but something had changed in Silvana since her mother died. He couldn't quite define it, but something about her reminded him of Mistress Sara. Whatever it was, it spoke to something deep inside him that knew she wasn't a woman he should disobey.

So he headed home, to find Gojko had gone out, so there was no one to question him gathering his meagre belongings into a sack, which he then slung over his shoulder as he headed back to the church.

The benches where Mistress Sara and the other council members sat during mass had been moved aside, so only the stone floor came between Raphael and the altar where Father Fazzio stood. The children who'd already arrived – and yes, some of them were definitely children, for the youngest could not have been a day more than six years old –

stood huddled in the corner nearest the door, half hidden behind the holy water font.

Raphael waited a while before Tobias finally returned, with a frown upon his face and a bulging sack in each hand. When they were younger, Raphael might have taunted him for having so many things. Now, he was torn between bitterness and embarrassment that he'd even been tempted to say something so petty. Whatever Tobias had, he would gladly share, if Raphael had need of it, and if Raphael ever had anything worth sharing, he'd do the same for Tobias.

"What's wrong?" Raphael asked instead, when his friend's frown only deepened.

"I couldn't find Mother. She wasn't at home, and the fire had almost died out. It's not like her…"

Raphael shrugged. "Maybe she had to go help someone, right after the vigil, and she didn't have time to go home or mend the fire. It's not like we'll need it tonight, for it's still summer. Ah, so that's why Silvana said she'd tell her about Father Fazzio's crusade — perhaps she knew where your mother went, and she's gone to find her."

Tobias relaxed. "You're probably right. It's just…Mother worries so, and I hate to worry her if she returns and I'm not home. She – "

Father Fazzio coughed loudly, drawing all eyes to him. "Come closer, children. Elder Ahab has something to tell you."

Between his red eyes and pale face, or what little Raphael could see of it over the handkerchief clamped to his mouth and nose, Ahab looked very sick indeed.

"Come closer," Father Fazzio said again.

They only huddled closer to each other in the corner.

Raphael sighed and stepped forward, until he stood as far from Father Fazzio and Elder Ahab as Tola had allowed to him to stand before stopping him.

Would two yards be enough to save him from the plague?

The others seemed to think so, as they

clustered around him. Only Tobias stood at his side – everyone else stayed behind them.

"Elder Ahab?" Father Fazzio prompted.

Ahab coughed into his handkerchief before he spoke. "We have been blessed by the Lord, blessed as no other town has been. And if we are to thank Him properly for this blessing, it must be with grateful hearts that fully accept Him and all he offers us. He sent us a sinner whose soul is so heavy, it is a wonder he can walk beneath the weight of such evil.

"But we will see through his evil, and turn it into good! My Ysabel…poor, sweet, innocent Ysabel, who surely dwells with the angels now, died to save us from our sins, so that we might see the truth. That the sinner among us also will be our guide to salvation!"

Raphael struggled to keep a straight face. Ysabel, may God rest her soul, was not the second coming of Jesus, and the pied ratcatcher was hardly the devil. Mistress Sara would not have engaged his services if he was an evil man.

Perhaps this madness was a blessing, taking the minds of those with the plague so that they slipped into death unknowing, not fearing their fate…

"This assassin, this Zoticus, will be brought to see that only two choices lie before him. He can lead a crusade so that his sins, grievous though they are, will be forgiven, or he can be executed immediately, and his soul will go straight to hell.

"And you, the innocents of Mirroten, will go with him to remind him that it is not just himself he saves, but all of you, and the Holy Land itself!" Ahab flung his arms wide, gazing rapturously at the rafters, as if waiting for heaven to rain something down on him.

Tobias folded his arms across his chest. "I can't leave the village, let alone go all the way to the Holy Land. Mother will never allow it. And who would look after the goats, Uncle?"

Ahab stared at Tobias, a tear trickling from one red-rimmed eye. "I fear Sara has fallen under his evil spell already, but she will be made to see the truth. You must stay here until she does. You will be safe here in the church – the devil can't touch you here." He stared at them for a moment, then added, "You will all stay here, lest your families who have also fallen under his spell try to dissuade you from your calling. You will not leave this church until you depart on your most holy crusade!"

Raphael wet his lips. "Sure, Elder Ahab. We'll stay here and pray. Tobias and I will see to it. You should…go and rest. Father Fazzio, too. We will keep vigil." At least until no one was watching, and then they'd make good their escape.

"Such a good boy! Father Fazzio, is he not a good boy?" Ahab beamed.

Father Fazzio frowned. "I feared he might have been led astray by the carnal wiles of the witch girl, but perhaps you are right, and he is redeemable, after all. Yes, it is most fitting. You shall remain here, in prayer, until it is time to leave."

Raphael's blood boiled. The carnal wiles of

the witch girl? How dare the priest talk about his betrothed like that!

Tobias kicked him. "Thank you, Father. Get some rest. Raphael and I will watch tonight."

The priest and the elder exchanged a brief, muttered conversation that Raphael couldn't quite make out, until both men nodded.

"I've taught you well, Tobias. Now, it is your turn to lead everyone, for while the assassin will be your guide, everyone here looks to you. Do not disappoint me," Ahab said. He swept out of the side door of the church, followed by the priest.

Raphael didn't dare breathe until he heard the door close behind them both.

He turned to Tobias. "Right, wait until we're sure they've gone, and then you go peek outside to see if there's anyone who will see us sneak out."

Tobias nodded. "We can't go on a crusade. We'll go somewhere else instead."

The church doors slammed shut, followed by the ominous scrape of the heavy bar being dragged across the doors.

Little Bernard burst into tears. "They've locked us in!"

Tobias and Raphael checked all the doors, but the boy was right. They were locked in.

"What do we do now?" Tobias asked, keeping his voice low.

It didn't matter. Too many worried eyes were watching, ears straining to catch every word. In the absence of Mistress Sara and the rest of the Elder Council, they looked to Tobias to lead them. And when Tobias deferred to Raphael, as if being taller and older by a few years was enough to make him a wise leader…

Raphael managed a weak smile, as he might for a patient he did not dare tell they were dying. "We do what we said we'd do – we pray. Pray that we find a way out of this, and survive the plague."

Six

Honking and flapping and splashing. Danger. Swanhild woke in panic, her only desire to take flight. Yet with the other swans crowding around her, wings beating and ready to buffet her, there was no escape. She didn't understand. This drift of swans had tolerated her for as long as she could remember – why were they driving her out now?

Too close…too many…no space…she could scarcely move without hitting another bird. Could no longer open her wings because there were too many other bodies in the way.

She squirmed, trying to get out from under the writhing mass of feather encased flesh. Swanhild managed to make her way to the top of the pile, extended her wings, tensing to fly away, when it hit her. A weight that would not let her go.

The other swans panicked, attempting to escape from the weight, and she fell, her feet sinking into the muddy river bank.

A net. Hunters – one, two, three. Danger.

She recognised that much, but when she tried to bite her lip to activate her magic, she could not. No amount of biting drew blood from her beak, and try as she might, the magic would not work. If there was a way to escape, she could not find it – through magic or otherwise.

She opened her mouth to scream, but her despairing honk was only drowned out amid the cacophony from at least a dozen other birds who could not possibly understand what had befallen them.

To be saved from the plague, only to die to hunters? But swans were under the Queen's protection. They couldn't hunt her. This was treason.

Swanhild flapped and fought, not caring whether she hit hunter or swan, her intent only to break the net and free them all, until one of the hunters threw a blanket over the net, and darkness smothered her senses.

Seven

Raphael waited until most of the children had fallen asleep before he pulled Tobias aside. "Did any of what Elder Ahab and Father Fazzio said make sense to you?"

Tobias shook his head. "What I've heard about the last crusade was that it was a failure. Sending children to the Holy Land…it's madness, is what it is. I mean, if it was you, and me, and maybe some of the others who are almost men, maybe we could join someone else's crusade, but…even if everyone in Mirroten went, it would not be enough to fight an army. The last crusade was full of seasoned knights, and most of those never made it home!"

Through his mother, Mistress Sara, Tobias heard much news from the outside world. Raphael knew next to nothing about crusades, except that he never wanted to go on one. What use was an apothecary in battle?

"Mistress Tola said we should leave Mirroten. Go up to the mountains. Maybe even to the monastery," Raphael said. "To keep us safe from the plague."

Tobias made a rude noise. "You and me, monks? I don't think so. My mother would never let me. And you…aren't you going to marry Swanhild? When you ever find the courage to ask her, that is!" He gave Raphael a playful punch.

Raphael rubbed his arm. Tobias was stronger than he'd realised – neither of them were children any more. "She's already gone, because her mother told her to." He couldn't bring himself to tell Tobias that Tola had turned her into a swan. "If we don't follow after her, we might be too late, and catch the plague. It's here already, Tola said. Ysabel had it, and her father, and Father Fazzio, too. Maybe that's why he's gone crazy. Does plague addle your wits?"

Tobias shrugged. "How should I know? You're the healer. I herd goats. Now, if you ask me about the ailments a goat can catch, I can talk about them all day. Put you right to sleep, too."

"Maybe that's not a bad idea. Sleep, I mean, not goat stories. Father Fazzio will be back on the morrow, and we must not get too close to him, especially not if he has the plague. Perhaps we can distract him, while the others escape, and we can catch up."

Tobias nodded. "It's a long journey up to the monastery. It takes Gojko weeks, usually. We'll need plenty of rest, for we'll be carrying the younger ones by the end. We'll need pack animals, supplies for the journey…and what about when we get there? What's it like?"

It had been years since Raphael had visited the monastery with Gojko, but he doubted it had changed much. "They have just enough for their needs. No more. The lands belong to Mistress Sara, so that's all they are allowed to take. Sometimes they fast for holy days, so there's no food but what we bring for ourselves. I wouldn't even know how much food to take for us, let alone everyone…"

"Mother will know. When we go, we must take her. No one will go hungry with Mother in charge," Tobias said.

Raphael could not argue with that. Mistress Sara had arranged for his apprenticeship after his parents died, so he knew firsthand how she cared for those who had nothing and no one.

"In the morning," Raphael said. "In the meantime, we get some sleep, so we're ready to outfox Father Fazzio when he comes."

"Good night!" Tobias said.

Raphael replied in kind, but he knew sleep

would struggle to find him that night. His thoughts flew with Swanhild, wondering where she was, what she was doing, and whether she was thinking of him. Whether she'd come back.

She had to. They were betrothed. She had to come back and keep her promise. Or else…what had he left to live for?

They would share a thousand days like today. No, more. He would not let it be their last day together. He and Swanhild would marry, and Mirroten would one day be safe again. He just had to survive until that day.

Eight

Swanhild wasn't sure she wanted to open her eyes. Wherever she was, it smelled like a henhouse that had been ravaged by foxes – all feathers and fear, floating over the stench of sour sawdust.

"You have your money. Now go."

The ground swayed beneath Swanhild, like she was aboard a boat and not on solid ground at all. Soft bodies tumbled against hers, warm and limp in unconsciousness. Then she was falling, along with them, before the thud to earth knocked the breath from her.

Now she opened her eyes, to find herself in a stable of some sort, like the low-roofed lean-to shacks the poorer people of Mirroten used to house their goats at night.

An enormous man in rough clothing stood over her, holding a crate bigger than he was.

Swanhild tried to push herself to her feet, but her hands felt peculiarly powerless today. Somehow, she managed to stand upright, but she barely came up to the man's waist. She glared up at him, and tried to say, "I don't know what you think you are doing with me, but I swear you will regret it." But all that came out was an angry hiss.

She'd made her point, though – the man dropped the crate and seized a pitchfork, pointing the tines at her.

Someone laughed – a giant standing behind Pitchfork Peasant. "That one reminds me of your wife. Maybe she'll do for the Queen's dinner."

The man with the pitchfork advanced, driving Swanhild back. "No, she's half-starved. Better to pick a plump one for the Queen, and fatten the rest for later."

The second giant leaned down. "This one, I think." He lifted a limp, feathered body from the pile, his meaty hand clenched around the swan's neck. The bird began to awaken at his touch, its wings unfolding, but the man tucked it firmly under his arm, preventing its flight. He carried it outside. A moment later, Swanhild heard the thwack of an axe hitting wood.

Then the giant returned, holding the now headless bird by its feet, so that blood dripped from the severed neck onto the earth.

"Scatter some grain for them, then shut the door. The sooner we're done for the day, the sooner we can go to the kitchens for dinner," he said.

The pitchfork man did as he was bid, leaving Swanhild alone with the darkness, her only companions the swans that had begun to rouse at the prospect of food.

None of them seemed perturbed by the death of one of their number. Perhaps the birds were too simple minded to understand the danger they were in.

But Swanhild was not simple-minded. She had little appetite for grain, either, not if it meant fattening them to be feasted upon.

She settled in the darkest corner of the tiny stable, the furthest place from the door, desperately praying she would escape before the same dark fate befell her.

Nine

Only eleven swans remained, oblivious to their impending doom as they gobbled up the grain on the ground. She'd tried to tell the others the dangers they faced, but the language of swans was much simpler than that of humans, and her loud honks had only conveyed that there was danger, not the how or why or even what it might be. She'd flown into a rage then, honking and flapping at them to drive them away from the food, but the foolish birds had then decided she was the danger, to be driven off with beaks and wing buffets until she took refuge in her dark corner, stinging in so many places from the feathers she'd lost in the altercation.

Well, if the stubborn birds attacked the only person who wanted to save them, perhaps they deserved to die. But Swanhild was determined to live, so that she might return home, where Raphael waited.

Several days ago, Swanhild had given in to her hunger pangs and eaten sparingly, so while the stupid birds gorged themselves, she alone heard the approaching footsteps. Swanhild tucked herself into the corner behind the door.

It had to be the butcher, coming to kill another bird for the kitchen. He always came after the birds had been given their evening meal, standing in the doorway as he decided which bird he wanted, before swooping in to seize his hapless victim. He'd shut the door behind him, but it was not thick enough to stop Swanhild from hearing the bird's last, panicked moments, before the thwack of the axe ended the poor creature's suffering.

She had planned this for days, but some instinct told her this was the moment she would put her plan into action. Her instincts had never been wrong in the past, and she had to trust them now, for they were all she had.

The door swung open, and a shadow blocked the afternoon light.

Swanhild crouched even lower, willing him not to notice her, as one of the other birds unknowingly enjoyed its last meal. They might not have the wits to save themselves, but their sacrifice today might save her life.

The butcher made his choice, a swan so greedy it had flopped down in the middle of the grain, eating everything within reach of its long neck. He stepped inside the stable and reached down to collect his prey.

Swanhild saw her chance, and darted for the door. She exploded into sunlight, blinded, but she didn't stop. She had only to run and flap her wings fast enough, and she'd be free.

Faster, faster, she'd never flapped so hard in her life, but desperation drove her. She had to fly, had to fly…Her wings caught the breeze and she nearly cried as her feet left the ground. Higher, higher…

She collided with something that said, "Oof!" as her wings wrapped around the unexpected obstacle. Together, they fell, with most of Swanhild on top, but one of her wings trapped underneath whoever she'd hit.

She squirmed and honked and struggled to get free, but then an arm wrapped around her. "You will do nicely," a female voice said.

Then Swanhild's head was enveloped in a cloud of sweet-smelling dust. She sneezed – once, twice, three times – but still those arms held her fast.

"No. Must…get…free…" Swanhild swore she was the one speaking, but it wasn't her voice saying the words. How…

But darkness lurked amid the dust, stealing Swanhild's senses and her hard-won freedom in one swoop.

Ten

Scraping and swearing roused Raphael from a weary doze. Tobias, the lucky bastard, was still snoring, though most of the others were on their way to awake.

Raphael gave Tobias a shake. "On your feet. They're coming, and we need to be ready."

"Ready for what?" one of the younger girls asked. In the dim light, Raphael couldn't be sure who she was.

"Tobias and I will distract them. When I

give the signal," Raphael demonstrated, "I want you to sneak out behind them, and get as far from the church as you can. Get to the mill, hide in the cellar there if you can. Wait for Silvana, or one of us, before you show yourselves. We'll take you somewhere safe, or Silvana will."

Most of them nodded.

"What if Mistress Sara comes?" the little girl with the questions persisted.

Raphael and Tobias exchanged a glance. Tobias's mother was a law unto herself.

This time Tobias answered, "Then you do whatever Mistress Sara says. Like you would any other day. Mistress Sara will keep us safe."

Raphael dearly wanted to believe it. Mistress Sara would do anything to keep the people of Mirroten safe. How, then, had the plague managed to arrive, despite her best efforts to prevent it?

The church doors flew open, and sunlight streamed in, haloing a lone man.

Raphael stood and squinted at the

silhouette. He didn't look like Ahab or Father Fazzio.

"That's not Mum," Tobias whispered, sounding disappointed.

The man moved, and Raphael glimpsed his face.

"It's Master Zoticus, the assassin," Raphael hissed. "Stay as far from him as you can. Don't move unless we give the signal. Until then, stay behind us."

Tobias swallowed, then looked at Raphael. Together, they stepped forward, neither wanting to break the silence.

Finally, Tobias said, "You may tell Elder Ahab that our vigil has not changed our resolve. We will not go with you on a crusade to the Holy Land."

Raphael hoped the assassin couldn't hear the quiver in Tobias's voice.

"Good," Zoticus said. "Because one crusade is more than enough for any man. I'll not be going on another. Anyone with any sense will not be heading for the Holy Land, but in the opposite direction. Up into the mountains, maybe, until the plague has passed."

Wait…what?

Raphael glanced at Tobias, who was too busy frowning at Zoticus to notice.

"You mean on a pilgrimage, to see some holy relics?" Tobias asked.

"Like the Cloister of the Holy Innocents? To see the jewel encrusted skeletons?" Raphael blurted out.

Now Tobias looked at him. "You've been there?" Naked envy coloured his tone.

Of course, that only made Raphael uncomfortable. Tobias was the one with everything, while Raphael was just an orphaned apprentice. That he could possibly have done something that inspired jealousy in Tobias, of all people… "Master Gojko journeys there once a year to trade herbs. They have some rather unusual ones that only grow high in the mountains, and because the Rialto traders can't go any further up the river, he buys extra to take to the Cloister. I used to go with him when I was younger, but now he leaves me to tend the shop while he's gone."

There. That should explain why Raphael had never mentioned it to his friend. Something so long ago, barely half remembered, hadn't been important enough to talk about until now.

"Could you take us there?" Zoticus asked, his gaze almost painfully sharp as he directed it at Raphael.

Raphael stared at his feet, wishing he'd paid better attention. "Maybe. Once you're on the right road, it's hard to get lost." Actually, the monastery would be the perfect place to flee to – far and fast, like Tola had said. "Why? Who's going to the monastery? It'll be autumn soon, and the high passes won't be open much longer. One decent snowfall and you're stuck there until spring." And safe from the plague, though not from assassins. Surely Zoticus had no intention of hiding in a monastery, though. Did they even allow assassins in such a holy place?

Zoticus didn't seem worried. "We all are, if we want to survive this plague."

So the assassin would be coming. Raphael didn't see how he could stop him, so he would have to resign himself to the man's presence.

But Tobias ruffled up like an angry rooster. "Why should we go anywhere with you? This is our town. We're not rats, to be driven out and drowned."

The assassin winced.

Ha, he was human enough to be hit by that barb, at least.

Then his eyes became steely again. "Because Lady Sara told me to take you."

Lady Sara?

Raphael met Tobias's eyes. No, he hadn't missed the title, either. That meant Zoticus knew Sara owned Mirroten, but was not familiar enough with her to know to drop the title. Maybe this was his mistaken way of trying to curry favour with her. Assassin or not, he'd seen how the man behaved toward her in the council meeting. He'd entered her service willingly, even if he wasn't entirely happy with her current orders.

Tobias lifted his hand to make the signal to the others, his eyes asking the question of Raphael.

But Raphael shook his head. All that Zoticus had said made sense, and it would be wiser to work with him than disobey Tobias's mother. If he was wrong... "You take it up with her. I wouldn't dare argue with Mistress Sara," Raphael said.

Tobias was reluctant, but finally he nodded. "I'd better get the goats. I'll never hear the end of it if I leave them behind." He dashed off.

The assassin stared after him. "Do you think he'll come back?"

Raphael couldn't suppress a grin. "Of course. Tobias said he was going to get the goats. It might take a while to get them all moving, but even he knows better than to cross his mum." And that should be warning enough to tell Zoticus that he shouldn't cross Mistress Sara, either.

The assassin nodded, as if he'd gotten the message. "Take everyone here down the road to the first traveller's camp to wait for me. We'll meet you there, with or without the goats," Zoticus said. He strode off after Tobias.

The others looked at Raphael. Somehow, he'd been left in charge.

"Right, gather your things. Don't leave anything behind, because it might be a while before we can come back. We're going on a pilgrimage," Raphael said. He hoped he managed to sound more excited than he felt. Because if any of the others knew about the emptiness inside him now Swanhild was gone…they wouldn't follow him anywhere.

Eleven

"No, you must lift the bread to your mouth, not bring your face down to the food!" The smack of flesh hitting flesh, before a yowling wail filled the air. "You will not eat unless you do it properly, or the King will know. No!"

Something felt wrong, Swanhild was sure of it, though she did not know what. She rested on softness, not the earth of that tiny stable or even her straw mattress at home. Only Mistress Sara had such a mattress, filled with feathers instead of straw. But the voice she heard did not belong to Mistress Sara, or anyone else Swanhild knew.

"You must learn, or you will not eat at all!" Another slap, followed by a longer wail.

Swanhild doubted Mistress Sara had ever struck anyone in her life. And she would give anyone in Mirroten the food from her own plate, rather than let them go hungry.

Even the thought of bread set Swanhild's stomach grumbling. Too long, she'd subsisted on the smallest specks of grain. If there was bread about, she was too hungry to resist.

She rose. Stone walls surrounded her on all sides, with the floor and ceiling made of the same grey stone. Beds were lined up against the wall behind her, with the rest of the room empty but for a table with benches on either side. Blank faced children sat along the benches, tears dripping from reddened eyes, as a long-necked woman towered over them from the head of the table, her arms folded across her chest, her glare enough to wither the smile off anyone's face.

Not that Swanhild had smiling in mind. Her sole desire was escape. While the woman was occupied with her children, perhaps Swanhild could reach the door and…

An arm wrapped around Swanhild, yanking her back. "And where do you think you're going?" the mother asked.

Swanhild was no child — not any more. She'd be a mother herself, soon after she and Raphael married. So she turned and returned the woman's glare. "I am going home. I do not belong here." Then she reached for the door.

Swanhild's hand stretched out — a real hand, not a wing — and surprise froze her for a moment. The moment was long enough for the woman to seize her by the ear and drag her over to the children's table, where she was forced to sit on the end of the bench.

"This is your home now, and you belong with me. You are my daughter, and you will behave properly — you all will! — or I shall find other swans that deserve to be princesses, and you shall be killed for the table, as you deserve."

The children wept and wailed, but Swanhild remained stony. This woman surely had to be the Queen, but if she was, the Queen had taken leave of her senses. "How could we possibly be your children?"

The Queen slammed both hands on the table. "I brought my true children here, to the King's hunting lodge, to keep them safe from the plague ravaging the countryside. Their stupid nurse, may the devil scourge her for eternity, permitted them to play on the beach by the lake, where infected rats had washed up. Having seen the priest burying bodies in the churchyard, they played at funerals themselves, burying the plague rats like common gravediggers. One by one, they sickened and died, followed by their fool of a nurse. I bore the King fifteen children, and I've outlived them all. Well, I will not bear him any more, nor will I be executed for treason, which he will surely do if he finds out what happened.

You will all be his children, or some other swans will take your place. You will behave as befits royalty, and you will live in luxury, or you shall die."

The Queen had gone mad with grief, Swanhild decided, but that didn't make her any less dangerous. A woman who had lost everything feared no consequences any more.

Swanhild wanted to ask a hundred, nay, a thousand questions, but the Queen's brittle composure threatened to crack at any moment.

"You will eat your dinner, and you will sleep. I shall see you in the morning," the Queen said, sweeping out of the room.

Swanhild heard the clunk of her barring the door on her way out. Her gaze swept the room, landing on a bronze mirror she hadn't noticed before. A mirror that showed a reflection very unlike her own, yet it moved as she did. She'd gone from her full grown self to a slip of a girl, budding breasts only just beginning to poke at the front of her gown. Only her eyes gave her away, for they weren't filled with the blank despair the other children shared. No, her eyes held dark foreboding, because every moment she stayed in this form, she committed treason with each and every breath. Pretending to be a noble, let alone a princess, was punishable by...actually, she wasn't sure what happened to them. It had to be bad, though, for no one dared do so.

Until now.

Then again, was it not treason to disobey the Queen, too?

Swanhild slumped in her seat and reached for the bread. She ate without tasting it, praying that she would survive the Queen's subterfuge, long enough to escape and return home to Raphael.

All the swan princesses' eyes turned to her, watching as she ate. Then, almost as one, they took some bread and joined her in her meal.

Twelve

The Cloister of the Holy Innocents soared high above them, a castle that might be impregnable if it closed its gates. But just like in Raphael's memory, the gates stood wide open, ready to welcome travellers and pilgrims alike. He remembered the place a-bustle with monks in their robes, doing whatever chores they'd been assigned for the day.

But now…he saw no one.

Someone shouted for a healer, and Raphael

turned to offer his assistance, only to be forced aside as Master Zoticus, still shouting, bulled past him into the great hall, carrying someone.

Raphael headed toward the herb gardens, and the back door to the kitchen, where he knew the still room was located. If there was a healer here, that's where he'd find them.

He found the still room well stocked, but empty of anyone but himself. From the dust on the workbenches, it looked like they'd left some weeks ago, and not returned.

"Raphael! There you are. You must come to the great hall at once. Master Zoticus wants you." Silvana beckoned.

"Master Zoticus the assassin wants me? But I'm just an apprentice apothecary. He can't possibly…" Raphael began.

"He wants a healer, and you're the best we've got. Come on!"

A good healer didn't go in blind. Perhaps some of the herbs in here could help. "What's the matter? Who's injured?"

Silvana swallowed, looking pale. "It's

Mistress Sara. She's coughing a lot, and Master Zoticus just put her to bed in the best bedchamber. Come with me, I'll show you."

Raphael's mind went blank. Not Mistress Sara. They couldn't lose Mistress Sara! He hurried to catch up with Silvana.

The best bedchamber was larger than his parents' house had been, with a massive bed that held Mistress Sara.

The assassin stood beside her, his expression full of dark shadows.

"I've brought Raphael." Silvana shoved him forward. She said something about dinner and departed, leaving him alone with the assassin and Mistress Sara, who looked weaker than he'd ever seen her.

He swallowed. If he was indeed the best healer they had, he'd do everything in his power to help her. They were lost without Mistress Sara.

"I found the stillroom. There are many herbs hung up there, most of which I recognise, and shelves full of jars that could contain anything. It will take some time, but within a few days, I should be able to make something to help Mistress Sara. What would be best for her cough is oil of rue, but that will take weeks..." He'd set to work straight away. The sooner he started, the sooner he would have what he needed. Unless he was very lucky and there was some in the still room already…but he'd have to search the place thoroughly if he had any hope of finding it.

The assassin pulled out a bottle that looked like it had come from Tola's shop. Yes, the label was written in Swanhild's own hand. He held the bottle over Mistress Sara's lips for the briefest moment, before corking it.

For one dreadful moment, Raphael wondered if he'd just witnessed the assassin poisoning Mistress Sara, and whether he'd be next.

But Swanhild would never have sold poison to an assassin. Something dangerous, perhaps, but he'd only given Mistress Sara the tiniest amount, as if he knew what dose to use safely.

Was the assassin a herbalism student, too?

The assassin – nay, Master Zoticus, for the man had a name and he'd best get used to using it, if they were to live in the same castle for some time – Master Zoticus stared at him for a moment, as if wondering why he was still there.

Raphael wondered the same thing. His stare was more than a little intimidating.

"Do what you can," Zoticus said, tapping the bottle. "I have enough oil of rue to do for some days yet."

Raphael nodded. "I'll see what I can find in the stillroom, and distil some more, as soon as I   can."

He hurried back to the stillroom. If Mistress Sara's life depended on his skills, he'd best take a full inventory of the stillroom by nightfall, before the contents of Swanhild's bottle were gone.

He sighed, wishing with all his being that Swanhild was here beside him. No one brewed potions as skilfully as she did – it was her they wanted, not him. But she was far away, likely flying through the air or drifting across a lake, safe with not a care in the world.

Thirteen

"You are a princess, not an animal! Lift the cup to your lips to drink!" the Queen scolded, cuffing the child so hard, the girl's nose went into her drink and she inhaled some of it. Coughing and spluttering, she overturned the cup, and soon all of them were splashed with water. Not to mention the nearly untouched food on the table.

"What is wrong with all of you? Why are you not eating? This is a feast fit for the King

— how can you not eat it? The servants are starting to say how strange you are. If they suspect..." the Queen continued, shaking her finger at them all.

Swanhild shook her head. If she, a human turned into a swan, had trouble understanding the Queen's constantly changing demands, what hope did these ordinary birds have? No wonder they would not eat or drink, if they were to be beaten for doing so. Beating children was bad enough. To beat innocent birds...birds who were supposed to be under her protection...

Swanhild snapped. She jumped to her feet. "Would you eat, if you were confined to this chamber instead of soaring through the skies, or drifting through the cool waters of a lake, catching your own meal?"

The Queen squinted irritably at her. "I've told you many times. If you cannot behave, I will find other, more pliable..."

"No, you won't," Swanhild said. "We're wild birds, used to being free. To be kept within these walls will kill us, and every other creature you transform into copies of your children. You must see this is foolish. You must set us free. Free to fly again, and feed as swans do!"

Not that she wanted waterweed, for she was growing quite partial to the cakes the Queen commanded the kitchen castle to make for her children. But the other birds were growing painfully thin…

"If you could fly, would you want to be confined so?" Swanhild persisted. She sensed a change in the Queen's demeanour, a slight slump of her shoulders, but the Queen's mood was as changeable as the wind, so it might mean nothing. Or it might mean she'd find herself as the target for the Queen's wrath. So be it. At least she could defend herself, unlike the others.

"No. I can not fly again, but if I could…and even though I can't, I still…these walls…" The Queen's eyes shimmered, with what looked like tears. "Very well. When night falls, meet me at the top of the tower. All of you. If you are good, and eat your dinner, then perhaps I shall permit you to fly again."

With a swish of her skirts, she left the room, closing the door behind her. Before Swanhild could reply, she heard the scrape of the key in the lock, and the Queen was gone.

Swanhild slumped into her seat. The others just stared listlessly at the table, as if they had not understood the exchange. Perhaps they hadn't.

"Here," she said, reaching for some bread. "Hurry and eat before she comes back. Never mind how, just make sure the food is all gone. It's the only way for any hope of getting free."

Swanhild wanted to believe it, but by the time the Queen returned, she might have forgotten her promise, or the sight of them might make her lash out again. Still, she had to hold onto hope. She had to get home to Mirroten. To Raphael.

Fourteen

Raphael stood on the threshold of Mistress Sara's chamber, clutching the vials so tightly it was a wonder they didn't break, but he didn't dare enter.

Something about the way Master Zoticus leaned over Mistress Sara, his eyes closed but such an intent expression on his face, screamed that the assassin was using magic. Not that Raphael could sense the stuff the way Swanhild could, but he'd seen the look on her face when she fell into one of her finding trances, as she sent magic out searching for what she wanted.

Raphael had never heard of a male witch before. Like Swanhild and her mother, he'd only known witches who were women. But there was no mistaking the fact that Master Zoticus was using some sort of spell on Mistress Sara. Whether for good or evil, though...

If he was doing her ill, Raphael should interrupt him, and stop him if he could. But if he was casting some sort of healing spell, something that would help Mistress Sara, the slightest distraction might make the spell go awry, and Raphael would never forgive himself if Mistress Sara took injury because of him. And yet...

He wished Swanhild were here. She'd use her magic and search the assassin for evil intent, and know whether he was Sara's friend or her foe. After the council meeting, Swanhild had insisted they should trust Zoticus, for he meant them no harm, she'd said. She'd even sold him some of her oil of rue, when she knew just how much they'd need every drop over winter.

If she were here now, Swanhild would still say the same thing – to trust the assassin.

So Raphael forced himself to stand in the doorway and watch, as his master Gojko had commanded him to do when entering any sickroom.

Zoticus had his hand pressed against Sara's throat, but lightly, as though taking her pulse. If he'd meant to do her harm, that hand looked strong enough to strangle her, but he did not. He would not, for the way his other hand clasped hers spoke of affection, tender feeling, like a man might show for his unwell wife, as he worried for her wellbeing while the healer made his assessment.

Wait…Mistress Sara and Master Zoticus, a match? No, surely not! Mistress Sara was too old for such things, with her son Tobias nearly a man grown. She and the assassin might be friends, but to imagine Mistress Sara sneaking off into the forest with him, like Raphael did with Swanhild, well, the thought was simply absurd.

An unexpected chill made him shiver and look up to find the assassin's eyes on him. Cold and calculating, as though he could read Raphael's thoughts and did not approve of them. Most of the adults in Mirroten would have disapproved of what he and Swanhild did, but it wasn't his fault they weren't married yet. He'd have made her his wife years ago, if she'd only agreed back then.

"What is it, boy?" Master Zoticus asked.

Raphael held out the vials with a shaking hand, hoping they would be shield enough to protect him from the assassin's wrath. "I found some oil of rue in the stillroom. I do not know how well made or even how old it is, so I would advise caution, only a drop at a time. While you have the stuff Swanhild made, I would use that. In the meantime, I shall make some more, if you wish it, of course."

Zoticus nodded slowly. "How much longer did you have on your apprenticeship?"

"I had hoped…and my master said…that I would be good enough to become a master by year's end. The sooner the better, for I am betrothed to be wed, and Swanhild will not marry me while I am a mere apprentice. Or, at least, she won't…if…" Raphael trailed off, not wanting to finish.

"You're betrothed to the witch girl? I have not seen her since we left Mirroten. Where is she?"

Raphael swallowed. A man who could use magic and maybe even read minds would want nothing less than the truth, however strange it sounded. So, Raphael told him how Tola had turned Swanhild into a swan.

"And what of the mother?"

These words came even harder still. "Dead. She bled out from casting the spell on Swanhild. I tried but she would not let me help her. She said she was already infected with the plague."

Master Zoticus nodded. "A great pity, which will grieve Lady Sara. Does anyone else know about Tola and Swanhild?"

Raphael shook his head.

"Then I must ask you not to tell anyone. We managed to save few enough from Mirroten, and I'm sure all of them left someone behind whose fate they fear, but do not know. Faced with the certainty that their witch is dead, and likely others with her, may be more than they can withstand. Let their fate remain a mystery, until it is safe to return to Mirroten."

Raphael did not want to agree. He rarely kept secrets from Tobias, or Silvana, and to be forced to hold this weight of grief inside, it was like his parents dying all over again, and it was only a matter of time before he ran away into the woods to give way to that grief, just as he had then. This time, though, there would be no Swanhild to come and find him, and without her, it was hard enough to see a way forward…

"You're needed here. You're the only healer they have. Well, the only one they trust, at any rate. I probably know more than you, but they know and trust you, more than they will ever trust me. With Lady Sara ill, it will be up to you, and Tobias and Silvana, to take charge of this place. To see in the last of the harvest, and ensure enough is stored to last everyone through the winter. I need you, to mix up whatever potions Lady Sara requires to bring her back to full health. Her recovery will take time, for she is not young any more."

"But I'm only an apprentice." Nowhere near skilled enough to save Mistress Sara or anyone else from the plague. "And no healer can save someone from the plague."

"Lady Sara does not carry the plague. It's an inflammation of the lungs that ails her. An affliction I can heal, but only with your help. Potions, herbs, poultices…will you make them exactly as I instruct you to, which whatever ingredients you can find? If you will help me nurse Lady Sara back to health, I will proclaim to anyone who will listen that you are no longer an apprentice but a master of your craft.

An apothecary in your own right, ready to set up your own shop and support your own family, when your swan girl returns. And she will, for birds are peculiarly immune to this plague. She will return, but not before it is safe for all of us to return to Mirroten again, and when she does, she will be looking for you. Will you be there when she does?"

It was Tola's dying wish, but Raphael could not deny that there was no future for him without Swanhild. She was everything to him, and he would do anything to ensure that they would meet again, and be wed, like she'd promised.

"Yes, Master Zoticus, I will do as you ask. Unless…unless Mistress Sara commands me to do otherwise. I can't disobey Mistress Sara."

To Raphael's surprise, the assassin laughed, and as he did, he became just a man, not some terrifying monster who might end his life in an instant. The man Swanhild had seen, and likely Mistress Sara, too, for Sara usually knew people better than they knew themselves.

"Yes, we would be fools indeed to even consider disobeying Lady Sara. A formidable woman indeed. The world would be a better place with more like her, but I fear she is unique. A woman to be treasured, as she deserves."

For a moment, Raphael thought he saw the same look in Zoticus's eyes that he felt in his own, when he gazed at Swanhild, before it was gone, so quickly he must have imagined it. He must have, for Master Zoticus was too old to fall in love with Mistress Sara.

"Is there anything else you would like me to bring you from the stillroom, Master Zoticus?" Raphael asked.

"Perhaps an infusion to help Lady Sara breathe. Something that will strengthen her, too," Zoticus said.

Raphael bowed, and headed back down to the stillroom to do his master's bidding.

Fifteen

Swanhild followed the Queen to the top of the tower, hearing the shuffle of the other swans' footsteps on the stairs below her. She wished she hadn't eaten so much, but if she was to escape tonight, best that she go with a full belly, for it wasn't as though swans could carry packs when they flew.

A chest sat in the shadows of the battlements, which the Queen knelt to unlock, before throwing the lid open to reveal…feathers.

No, not just feathers, Swanhild realised as the Queen lifted the first layer up high, but feathered cloaks, so artfully fashioned that when the Queen gave it a shake, it flared out and looked like wings in flight.

Surely she couldn't mean for them to don these cloaks and actually fly…

"My godmother fashioned these for me, each a little larger as I grew, until I reached the height I am now. They are all imbued with magic, transforming the wearer into a swan for as long as the full moon is in the sky. But should sunlight touch even a single feather, the entire cloak will erupt into flame, burning the wearer and sending them plummeting to earth and a painful death." The Queen gave the cloak one last shake, before sweeping it around the shoulders of the smallest swan child. She fastened the bone button at the child's throat, then stepped back. "There!"

There, indeed. The cloaked child flapped her arms, once, twice, three times, and they were no longer arms but wings, her neck stretching, stretching, as before Swanhild's eyes, the child turned back into a swan.

Swanhild wanted to weep. The bird looked so pathetically grateful to be herself again, but it was only for a night. By dawn tomorrow, they'd all be back to being children again, at the mercy of the mad Queen.

But for one night…she might go home to Mirroten, and at least see Raphael again.

"Wearing one of these cloaks, you may fly where you wish while the moon is in the sky, but you must return here to this tower before dawn, or you will die a fiery death. Do you understand?" the Queen said.

Swanhild nodded, and the others did, too.

"And when you return, you will be good little children, and make King Bela believe you are truly his daughters. If you behave yourselves, I will allow you to fly on the night of the next full moon, just like tonight, but only if you can convince the King. Can you do that?"

Swanhild doubted it. Anyone with eyes to see would surely notice that there was something odd about these children who did not speak or behave like anything but scared savages. And yet…if they did not agree, the others would surely die, and she would never see Raphael again…

"Yes, Your Majesty," Swanhild said.

"Yes, Mother," the Queen corrected.

Swanhild swallowed. If this was the Queen's price…so be it. "Yes, Mother."

She helped the Queen dress the others, until only she remained, with the largest cloak of them all. It was too big for Swanhild, for the Queen was far stouter than she, but she threw it about her shoulders anyway, fastening the clasp with feverish fingers.

Swanhild closed her eyes and stretched her arms out. She took a deep breath, flapped her arms once, twice, then lifted them a third time…

Tingling began in her fingers, spreading up her arms, before moving across her whole body. Lightness invaded her very bones, until she felt she might float away. This was nothing like her mother's spell, that first time, filled with shifting and strangeness and pressure. No, this was…magical, like stepping into a forest clearing and suddenly being enveloped in a shaft of sunlight, and the whole world seemed to effervesce like a complicated potion made just right.

Swanhild felt as if she could simply step off the top of the tower and float all the way down, feather light. She could. She would…

Almost without thought, she stepped up onto the battlements, arching her shoulders to spread her wings as wide as the crenelations would allow. The world…nay, the very universe demanded that she fly.

An updraft rising from the sun-warmed courtyard below beckoned, and Swanhild could not resist. She leaned forward and stretched out her wings.

The wind lifted her, like she weighed nothing more than a feather, and she floated for a moment before another updraft sent her higher still. With a cry of triumph, Swanhild soared, circling the tower far below.

From up here, she could see the shining expanse of the lake, with the moon's reflection laying out a path home to Mirroten. While the other swans spiralled upward toward her, Swanhild flapped her wings and arrowed toward the water.

She heard the others land in the lake behind her, in the shallows where the forest grew right down to the water's edge, and the waterweed was thickest. That would keep them occupied, while she headed for Mirroten.

Swanhild glided down in the lee of the dock, hoping the shadows would hide her from anyone watching the water. Swans might be under the Queen's dubious protection, but some of the boys in the village would happily chase and torment anything smaller or weaker than themselves, and not even a few strong wing buffets would deter those little brutes from their sport.

She waded ashore at the spot where Mercurio had set up his stall. Only scant days could have passed since he'd packed up and left, for she could still see the circles in the sand from the casks he'd used to prop up his counter. Either that or she'd been a swan so long that he'd had time to travel to Rialto and return.

It mattered not, she decided, as she strode across the sand to the grassy bank above. No one moved in the streets, and the nearby houses were dark. Was it so late in the evening? It could not be midnight yet. Or perhaps everyone was in the church, or the council hall…

Hope died a little when she reached the church, and a little more by the time she arrived at the darkened council hall. Everyone in the town was simply gone. Or dead from the plague…

No. Swanhild couldn't bear to even think it. She took flight across the lake, rousing the other swans from their post-supper roost and into the air alongside her, to fly back to the Queen and her tower.

Sixteen

"Tobias has asked me to take over Mistress Sara's care," Raphael found himself saying, the moment Master Zoticus stepped into the stillroom.

Zoticus did not look surprised, or even miffed that Raphael hadn't waited for him to ask. "Yes, he said as much to me. Locking the door to Lady Sara's chamber and placing his own body across the threshold every night is unnecessary, though. He is your friend.

Perhaps you should speak to him about it, and try to dissuade him?"

He already had, but Tobias wouldn't listen. He was so worried the assassin might hurt his mother, he was blind to what was really going on between them. Now Mistress Sara was awake, she'd made it perfectly clear that she had no problem allowing the assassin in her bedchamber.

So he'd gone to a greater power for help. "Silvana will do a better job, I think. She came asking for some special herbs, the sort girls use to prevent pregnancy, this morning. She said they were for someone else, but when I tried to tell her how much to use and when, she brushed me off, as though she knew what she was doing. She can't have been with anyone but Tobias, and she wouldn't…not outside Mistress Sara's door…"

Zoticus grinned. "Good man. Seeing as you're in the habit of making wise decisions today, I'm going to ask you to make another one. Given the improvement in Lady Sara's health, do feel that you could take on the responsibility Tobias has asked of you?"

Raphael's jaw dropped. "You mean…be Mistress Sara's healer, not just an apprentice? But you…"

"I believe you can do it, and your friend is struggling to step up and lead the people of Mirroten, as he must while his mother is still ill. If he no longer needs to worry about whether she will recover, it will set his mind at ease enough to focus on what is important – his real responsibilities. So, what do you say? Are you enough of an apothecary to do what is necessary?"

"I guess so…but if something were to go wrong, and Mistress Sara were to grow sicker instead of better…" He'd never forgive himself for failing her.

"Worry not, for I will be watching."

Raphael almost laughed with relief. A scant few weeks ago, such words from the assassin would have made him worry more than ever, but he thought he knew Master Zoticus well enough now to be sure the man was always watching. Watching like an eagle from its eyrie, scanning the landscape for suitable prey, but otherwise unruffled until its quarry caught its attention. Who his quarry was, Raphael could not be certain, but he was sure it was not himself, or Mistress Sara, or any of the people who'd come from Mirroten.

"Thank you," Raphael said.

"No, thank you. Lady Sara is much improved, and both she and I owe you our thanks for your skills in the stillroom. It takes a master to know one herb from another, how to prepare them, and to make sure the dose is right. When you return to Mirroten, and you wed your swan girl, you will have no problem supporting what I'm sure will be a large family with your burgeoning apothecary business."

A large family with Swanhild? Oh, he hadn't even dared hope…but…

"Do you think it will be safe to return soon?" Raphael asked eagerly.

Zoticus shook his head. "I am no expert,

but the witch was, and she said it might be years before it will be safe in Mirroten once more. We will not know until the monks return to the monastery. And when they do, you will be the first person I send to Mirroten, to see what you have left to go back to."

Swanhild, or so he hoped. He didn't dare think otherwise. She had to be there when he returned, or he had nothing left to hope for.

Seventeen

The next morning, as the other swan children dozed fitfully in the carriage on their way to court, Swanhild bitterly regretted her cowardice. She should have checked inside the houses. She might have been in the form of a swan, but that didn't make her any less of a healer, and if people were ill inside, she might have been able to help. Or…something. At least she would have known whether Raphael was alive or dead. Or Mother. Or if they were all simply gone somewhere safer.

She could think of nothing else as the Queen settled them into the royal nursery, where Swanhild had her hands full trying to train the other swan children to at least behave like children. They never spoke, but they seemed to understand her, though how, she did not know. Servants came and went, bringing food and clothes, or taking away laundry and dirty dishes, laying fires and sweeping away ashes. They didn't seem to mind the swan children ignoring them, which Swanhild found hard to believe. When she'd pointedly thanked one of the maids for clearing away after a meal, the girl had ducked her head, refusing to meet Swanhild's eyes, as she bobbed a curtsy before fleeing the room.

Perhaps it wasn't the swan princesses the maids feared, but the Queen, whose chambers occupied the lower levels of the tower that also held the nursery. A nursery that had become as much a prison as their chamber in the King's hunting lodge.

Swanhild lost count of the days, for they all blurred into one another, locked within stone walls, as they were. It felt like months before the Queen brought out her chest of feathered cloaks and summoned them to the top of this new tower.

But when Swanhild stepped out onto the battlements, her breath caught in her throat. This castle sat atop a mountain, topped by towers that soared up into the very clouds. She could see the whole valley below, the town spread out on both sides like the most marvellous children's toy, all the way to a line of mountain sentinels, armoured in stone and snow.

Home was on the other side of those mountains, she knew with a certainty that resonated deep down in her bones. Raphael lay in that direction, too, though whether he lived or not, she could not say. This time, if the Queen permitted her to fly, she would spend the night scouring all the houses in Mirroten, to see if Raphael or anyone else could be found.

Swanhild scarcely felt the wintry breeze as she arrowed over the mountains, toward the lake. Snow lay on the ground here, as smooth and untouched as though it was freshly fallen, though the icicles hanging from the eaves told a different story. The snow was untouched because no one had walked on it, for there was no one left to do so.

Still, she resolved not to waste what time she had in Mirroten. It took her some time to work out how to use her wings and beak to nudge open the door to her mother's house, but once she was in, the others were easier. There was no sign of Mother, and the other houses along the road were just as empty, all the way down to the mill. That's as far as she managed to get on that first night – it wasn't until spring had taken the town firmly in her grasp that Swanhild reached the final house in town she intended to check – the great house where Mistress Sara lived with her son, Tobias.

Like all the others, the house stood empty,

but it was the barn that drew Swanhild's attention the most. The two carts Sara usually kept there were gone, along with all her horses and their entire herd of goats. What a fool she'd been, checking all the houses instead of the barns…if the goats were all gone, they must have left with the people who owned them, or at least Tobias.

Swanhild wanted to laugh, but the only sound that came out of her beak was honking. Still, it was funny to think of Sara and Tobias, as distant from the Queen as chalk and chestnuts, for they would never strike an animal or a child, or lock one up for weeks at a time.

Wherever they had gone, she prayed that they were safe, from the plague and whatever else might befall them, and that they would return soon. For, despite a layer of dust, and the chill in the air, most of the houses looked like their residents had merely stepped out for a moment, fully intending to return.

And when they did, Swanhild would return,

too. She'd persuade her mother to reverse this spell so she might be herself again, and she'd marry Raphael, just like she'd promised.

She would, she swore softly to herself. For she could not bear to even think of a future without them.

Eighteen

When Silvana and Tobias moved out of the monks' dormitory they'd shared with the others, and Zoticus left the tower room to sleep in Mistress Sara's chamber, Raphael took the tower room for his own. Oh, he'd had offers from some of the girls, and if not for Swanhild, he might have been tempted, so it was best that he sleep alone, somewhere they would not find him. And if it had the best view of the gates and the road up the mountain, all the better.

He spent every spare moment up there, feeling like he, and not Zoticus, was an eagle in an eyrie, but in the end, it was Zoticus and Sara's daughter, a wilful little mite named Rossa, who saw the party of monks first.

Nevertheless, Raphael's longer legs carried him down to the bailey faster, so he was the one to tell Zoticus of their approach. Zoticus was already at the gates, as if he knew they'd be coming today, and his only response to the news was to tell Raphael to pack his things, ready to travel home to Mirroten.

The sun was still high in the sky when Raphael rode out of the gates on the back of the bishop's own palfrey, no less, for the bishop had no further need of the beast.

Raphael did not glance back, for he hoped to return with good news soon enough. Now, he set his sights firmly on Mirroten, and his reunion with Swanhild. He had a promise to Tola to fulfil.

Nineteen

"The king has summoned you! All of you! You must dress for court…and don't forget the crowns! They must wear their crowns!"

The Queen flew about, like a panicked bird not sure of the way out, slapping child and servant alike as she gave orders to everyone.

Fine gowns were found, then picked over, before being approved and dragged over the heads of swan princesses who'd begun to panic themselves in the pandemonium in the nursery.

The whole room was a froth of fur and silk and wool, with so many preservative herbs flying about that Swanhild had sneezed more than once, to the terror of the smaller girls.

Finally, it was Swanhild's turn to be dressed in her finery, a confection with so many layers of silk and lace, she worried the dress might try to fly away on its own, for the slightest puff of wind sent the skirts dancing.

"A crown! She must have her crown!" the Queen cried, and a circlet was pushed so forcefully onto her head, Swanhild's knees threatened to buckle.

While the Queen and two maids busied themselves, stabbing pins into her hair as they pulled it this way and that, Swanhild dared to look at the others. They were all dressed now, looking like the princesses the Queen pretended they were. Each girl wore a thin silver circlet with a jewel on her brow, which didn't look half as heavy as the crown weighing down her own head. Swanhild reached up to investigate…

"Don't touch it, you silly girl!" the Queen screeched, slapping Swanhild's hands away. "You'll undo all our good work, and the King is waiting!"

The Queen, dressed in her own finery and topped by a heavy crown that Swanhild suspected was a twin of the one on her own head, led the way to a hall so huge it could only be the King's throne room – as evident by the man seated on an ornate chair on a dais at one end.

When they reached the foot of the dais, the Queen halted, then hissed, "Bow before the King!"

Of course, none of the swan princesses had ever been taught to curtsy, so they merely stood there, looking confused, and not a little frightened at what the Queen might do to them.

The Queen uttered an oath under her breath, then began to clout each child over the head until they fell to their knees. By the time she reached Swanhild, she had already dropped into a deep curtsy, which she hoped looked as subservient as any maid.

"What's that one's name?"

Swanhild raised her head, to find the King pointing at her.

"That is Princess Odette, your oldest daughter," the Queen said.

"She will be sixteen this summer, yes?" the King asked.

Swanhild blinked in surprise. The child she'd seen in the mirror did not look anywhere near sixteen.

The Queen seemed to be equally unsettled. "She is still young, Your Majesty. Too young to leave the nursery, I am certain."

The King shook his head irritably. "No, I'm certain she is sixteen, at least. Born the same year as the Emperor's son and heir, though he would not consider a betrothal between them. It matters not. At Midsummer, she will wed Prince Tristan, and when I am gone, they will rule this kingdom together, as king and queen."

"But she is so young…"

"No younger than you were when we wed, Klava. Young enough to be fertile and give him many heirs to the throne, just as you have. Though I hope Odette and Tristan will at least have a son." The King's eyes seemed to accuse the Queen of some terrible crime, of failing to bear him a son.

If the King only knew that the sex of a child was determined by both parents, not just their mother…Swanhild couldn't help but grin.

"See? The girl approves. You know you are old enough to marry, do you not, Odette?" the King asked.

Curses – the King had seen and misinterpreted her smile. Oh well, better make the best of it. "If my betrothed stood here before me, I would gladly marry him today, Your Majesty," Swanhild said. Of course, she meant Raphael, not some northern prince, but the King wasn't to know that. She grinned even more widely. "And spend all night working on conceiving a son, of course." Or a daughter. Swanhild didn't much care about the sex of her first child with Tobias, as long as they spent plenty of time in bed together before the baby was born.

The Queen glared daggers at Swanhild, but the King merely laughed. "Daughter, you are exactly the sort of queen this country needs. Your mother would be wise to listen to you, child." He rose and made shooing motions. "Now, take the children back to the nursery. I will send for her when Prince Tristan arrives to take possession of his new bride."

The Queen turned her back on the King and swept out of the hall. "Come, children," she called.

Swanhild had the most peculiar urge to open her mouth and tell the King everything his wife had done, but she knew as well as the Queen did that pretending to be a princess was just as much treason as any of the Queen's crimes, and the result would be death, either at the Queen's hand or the King's.

Swanhild sighed. She'd have to find some

way out of here, before they forced her to marry Prince Tristan. Even if he was the handsomest, kindest, most skilled lover in all the world, she would never break her promise to Raphael.

Now she just had to find a way to keep her promise and her head.

Twenty

That night, Swanhild was surprised when the Queen led them up to the top of the tower, where the chest of feathered cloaks lay open to the starry sky. The moon had not yet risen, but the glow on the horizon signalled that it would appear soon.

Much like every other full moon night when she'd been allowed to fly, Swanhild helped the others into their cloaks until there was only one left for the Queen to hand to her.

Tonight, the Queen clutched it in her hands like she didn't want to let go.

"Odette, you must tell me something, and you must tell me the truth. Swear it!" the Queen said.

The Queen's madness had made her forget the girl before her wasn't really her daughter. Swanhild sighed.

"Swear you will tell me the truth!"

Swanhild wet her lips. This could not end well. "I swear it."

"You have already found a mate, have you not? One you fly to meet, every full moon?"

A mate? It was a strange choice of words, but if Raphael was anything, then yes, in the most animal sense, he was her mate, her partner in life, and when they finally said their wedding vows, it would be a mating, of sorts.

She'd sworn to tell the truth, but what would the Queen's madness make her do to Raphael, if he still lived? Swanhild could not place him at the mercy of this mad woman.

"Do your hearts beat as one? Have your

bodies already become one? Does your heart belong to him, and not some prince?" the Queen demanded.

Swanhild swallowed. "My heart belongs to someone who is not the prince the King wishes me to marry."

"I knew it! I will not let history repeat. I will not…" the Queen muttered feverishly to herself. She settled the last cloak about Swanhild's shoulders, as lovingly as if the girl had truly been her daughter. "Tonight, you must give yourself to him. The male who holds your heart. Give all of yourself, over and over, until there is no doubt in his heart or your own. Then, return here to tell me it is done. Only then can I set matters straight."

As if Swanhild could find Raphael in a single night, when she'd been looking for him since the day she first turned into a swan. So many months, with no sign of where he might be or if he was even alive. She opened her mouth to say something, anything, but before she could form the words, the Queen fastened the cloak clasp at her throat and the transformation silenced her.

So Swanhild gave the Queen a nod, before diving off the tower into the swirling winds that had carried the other swan princesses away to the lake.

Twenty-One

In all the years he'd lived there, Mirroten never looked so quiet as it did right now. Raphael half expected people to walk out of their doors, to greet him, but there was no one left. Every house stood empty, with neither a man nor a mattress to be seen.

He found the answer to the mystery in the churchyard. A massive mound rose on along the fence on one side, topped by a stone cross. Grass had grown over the top, withering to straw now after the warm summer. Someone had buried all those who'd perished of the plague some time ago, then left the town empty. Maybe even the monks who were, even now, settling in to the monastery that had sheltered them for so long.

Raphael had known the disease would take its toll, and immeasurable lives would be lost. He'd known, but…it hadn't really hit him until now, seeing that grave as big as a house, that was now home to Gojko and all the townspeople he'd tried to save from so many ailments over the years. Until the plague had come and wiped them all from the world.

He fell to his knees and wept. Wept for all those lost, unmourned until now. When their children returned to Mirroten, they would mourn them, too, but today, Raphael alone held that crushing weight of grief, and was forced to collapse beneath it.

Hours later, he staggered into the church, determined to light a candle for their souls. Flint, tinder, fire, and then finally a taper…it seemed such a tiny flame for so many souls, so after lighting one candle, he lit them all, every candle he could find in the church until the altar was a blaze of light. Even that wasn't enough, and Raphael stumbled out into the street again, looking to the skies for something, anything, a sign that this was all part of some plan, that so much sacrifice could not have come without some reward. Or why had so many died?

A gust of wind blew past him through the open church doors, snuffing all the candles out in one breath. Much like the plague had taken the lives of the people Raphael had tried to pray for, though the words would not come.

Wings flapped, high above. A flock of some night birds, ghostly white, drifted overhead, toward the lake.

Swans. They must be swans! Raphael's heart soared, and he sprinted for the beach.

Twenty-Two

Swanhild circled the town, looking once again for signs of life, like she did every time she came to Mirroten. All the snow had melted away in the spring thaw, and she knew as well as anyone in Mirroten that once the spring sun had dried the roads, they would show no footprints until the next autumn rains fell.

Just like every other night, the only light came from the full moon above.

Swanhild shook her head. The Queen was

mad, as she knew well. No matter how much she wished he was, Raphael wasn't here.

She coasted in to land, skimming the water as she slowed before settling in the shallows. If she'd known flying was so much fun, she might have asked Mother to transform her into a swan sooner. Or a more agile bird, like a falcon or something. When she saw her again, she would ask.

Once again she felt the urge to walk through town, checking her house and the apothecary shop, in the faintest of hopes that she might find some clue to where they'd gone. She knew there'd be none, for surely if there was anything to find, she'd have seen it by now, but hope burned eternal. She would walk the streets of Mirroten one more time.

She stepped out of the water, surprised to find that it was the same patch of shore where Mother had first turned her into a swan. Swanhild had the strangest sensation that if she but took off her cloak, she would be herself again, and the world would be as it was before.

So strongly did she feel it that she reached for her throat to unclasp her cloak, only to discover that her wings were useless. Hissing a curse, she set to work on the clasp with her beak. She could feel the bump where it should be, but no matter how hard she pecked and tore at it, it wouldn't budge.

She hissed again and set off for her mother's house. She'd find something there that would help her take her cloak off.

"Swanhild? Is that you?"

She turned, at the sound of a name she hadn't heard in far too long, from the lips of someone who couldn't possibly be...

"Raphael?"

Twenty-Three

A single swan stepped out of the water, walking up the beach with a measured step that reminded Raphael of Swanhild. This swan had a strange band about its head that gleamed in the moonlight, almost like a crown.

It unfolded its wings, feathers spreading like fingers as it reached for something on its breast. It tried a few times, but whatever it wanted to do, it appeared that it couldn't, and the frustrated bird hissed something that had to be a curse, exactly like Swanhild would.

"Swanhild?"

She'd twisted her head around to try to reach whatever it was that her wings couldn't grasp, so it took her a moment to right herself. One piercing eye regarded him as she honked softly three times.

"Let me help you with that," Raphael said to the swan, dropping to his knees before her. She spread her wings wide, as if warning him away. He half expected her to buffet him with her wings, like a normal bird would do, but instead she puffed out her chest, and touched the offending part with her beak. In the moonlight, he could see what looked like an ivory brooch, gleaming against her feathers. He fumbled with the clasp, wishing he'd thought to bring a lamp so that he might see better, but finally he managed to yank the thing free.

The swan flapped her wings, then uttered the most horrible cry. Her features blurred, before it was no longer a swan but Swanhild standing before him.

"Raphael! Are you really here?"

He had no words, but he could and did wrap his arms around her. His lips found hers, and he drank her in like the first draught he'd had in three years. Nay, in forever, for that's what their time apart had felt like.

They could not shed their clothes fast enough, and it was but the work of a moment before he felt her body against his on the sand, ready and willing and wanting. She pushed him onto his back, straddling his hips as she took him the way she liked best.

The heat of her around him, moonlight gleaming on her breasts as she rode him to the peak of her own pleasure, was more than he could bear, and his cry of joy mingled with hers as they came together.

Still breathless, she leaned forward to kiss him, then rose. "I want to do that again, and again, and again, until neither of us can walk any more. But next time, I want to do it in a bed."

Raphael grinned. "The only mattresses left

in town are the ones in Mistress Sara's house. I'm sure she would not mind."

Swanhild looked surprised. "She lives, then? And the others?"

Raphael nodded. "All the other survivors took refuge at the Cloister of the Holy Innocents, a castle high in the mountains. Not everyone survived, though. I'll show you tomorrow. Tonight it's just us here, and we can do as we wish."

"I wish to make love with you, to feel you inside me, until I forget everything else but you and me," Swanhild said.

Raphael laughed. "Then I will become as one of those desert djinn, and grant your wish, in one of Sara's soft feather beds."

"Oh, yes!"

Twenty-Four

When Swanhild awoke in an unfamiliar bed, her body ached in places she'd forgotten existed. And she could think of nothing but Raphael. His lips, his hands, his body, his voice…caressing her until she begged for more, for she would never ask him to stop. Such a beautiful dream…

"I brought your clothes. We left everything on the beach. Oh, and some water to wash with. I thought you might want to dress before

I showed you the churchyard."

She looked up, and he was there. "Every night, I dreamed of you, wishing you were there with me. Is it…are you…is it over now?"

He sat on the edge of the bed and leaned in to kiss her. His lips tasted salty-sweet, and she wanted…

"It is indeed over, my dearest friend, my only love, my soon to be wife. Come back with me to the castle, and we will make the priest marry us, so that we may do this again every night, and you need never dream of me again, for I will be right beside you, only a whisper away."

Tears sprang to Swanhild's eyes. The mad Queen had been right after all. Raphael was really here, and hers, and nothing and no one would ever part them again. Not king or queen or even her own mother.

"Is my mother…is she…?" Swanhild began, not sure how to finish.

"Dress, and I will show you," Raphael said.

He'd brought her the silk and lace court

gown, that decadent thing that seemed so out of place on her, or here in Mirroten. And yet, that's all the clothing she had, so she slipped it over her head, tying the many laces herself until it fitted her just as it had before the King. The crown lay beside her pillow, a heavy half circle of silver that rose up to a jewelled point in front. It belonged on a princess, not on her humble head, but she put it on anyway, for it would not do to lose such a valuable jewel, even in Mistress Sara's house.

Her shoes were silk court slippers, hardly suitable for Mirroten's roads, but they were better than going barefoot. Or being a swan.

She twisted her hair up onto the back of her head, pinning it to keep hair and crown in place, before venturing out to where Raphael waited.

His eyes lit up at the sight of her. "You look like a princess, or an angel. Having seen you naked, I had not thought you could ever appear more beautiful to me than that, but looking at you now…where did you find such a gown, Swanhild? Or that crown? Will you wear it to our wedding?"

So much to say, and Swanhild knew that once she started, she would not stop, but she did not want to tell her tale more than once. "First, show me to my mother. Then I will tell you both about the gown, and the crown, and my life as a swan."

Raphael nodded gravely, and led her to the church. To the rounded hill where once there had been flat ground, topped with a stone cross with edges so sharp they cut her fingers when she gripped it. Swanhild watched a blood droplet well from her fingertip, before closing her eyes and sending her magic sight out to find her mother.

The magic flew out wide, before coalescing back around Swanhild, sinking to the ground around her slippered feet. Then it sank into the mound, and she knew.

"My mother?" She let out a sob.

"I'm sorry, Swanhild. The spell she cast to turn you into a swan took too much out of her. She was already weak from the plague. After Ysabel, she was the second person in Mirroten to die. With her last breath, she made me promise to protect you, and I will. I swear I will."

A grave so large held more than one body – it must hold half the town, if not more. So many friends and their families, people she had known all her life. Gone.

Raphael took her in his arms as she wept for all she had lost. All they had lost. So much, so many, and yet they were still here…

And when she had cried herself out, she sat down with him and told her tale.

Twenty-Five

Somehow, while telling their stories, they'd managed to walk back down to the beach. There were no swans on the lake now – they'd evidently flown back to the Queen, to be safely inside by dawn. Some other swan princess would marry Prince Tristan now, Swanhild supposed, seeing as she wasn't going back. The prince wouldn't know the difference, for they'd never met, and the Queen surely wouldn't care, for she'd gone three years pretending swans were her children after the real princesses had died. The only person Swanhild really felt sorry for was the King, who evidently didn't know the death of their children had driven her mad.

And the swans. Not the brightest birds, but they didn't deserve to live out their lives as the Queen's captives. Someone should go to court and tell the King to let them go.

"Oh, here's your cloak, where we left it on the beach last night. I must have missed it when I collected the rest of your clothes. I'm never seen a feather cloak before. It looks like a great deal of work, every feather sewn to the cloth..." Raphael picked up the cloak and shook the sand off it.

Swanhild reached out to take it from him, then stopped. It was nearly noon, with not a cloud in the sky. Sunlight shimmered off the feathers, which absolutely did not melt or burn or do any of the things the Queen had said it would in the sun.

"That lying, scheming bitch," Swanhild breathed. "She held us prisoner in a cage of her own lies!" She took the cloak from Raphael and settled it across her shoulders. It was warm from the sun, but that was all. They could have escaped her at any time by simply not returning. The other swans still could, if she only told them.

But that would mean leaving Raphael.

Quickly, she told him what she'd come to realise.

"You must go, and save those swans. We've waited three years. What is a few more days?" he asked. "While you go back to save them, I will go get everyone and bring them back to Mirroten. When you return, we will have our wedding here, with all the town as our guests."

"Yes," she said, before doubt seized her. What if something went wrong? She did not want to wait another three years. "If I have not returned by the time you come back, come to court. Bring Mistress Sara, if you can. She will know what to say, and how to say it, to the King and the Queen. The King must know what she has done."

Raphael touched his lips to hers. "You will return, and we will be married. Nothing will go wrong. But if it does, I will challenge the Queen herself before I will let her keep you captive again." He fastened the clasp, and stepped back.

Magic tingled over Swanhild's body, as she transformed into a swan for what she hoped was the last time. Into the water she went, flapping her wings to generate enough lift to launch her into flight.

She circled around Raphael once, twice, three times, memorising his every feature as she prayed she would see him again soon, before she flew off.

Twenty-Six

The Queen was waiting at the top of the tower when Swanhild landed. But instead of unfastening her cloak, the Queen picked her up and carried her down the stairs to her chamber.

"I knew you would return, Odette. I knew! Tell me, did you mate? Did you mate for so long that you lost track of the time?"

Unable to say anything that wasn't a wordless honk, Swanhild simply nodded. The

Queen, married to a man she had no problem lying to, would not understand what it was share a love like the one she and Raphael had. And the joy of their lovemaking…even as a human, she did not have the words to express it so the woman would even have a hope of understanding.

"Then it is time I told you my tale. A tale of my mate, the mate who was stolen from me, by the man I was forced to marry," the Queen began.

Wait…what?

"When I was young, younger than you, a witch came to our court. An enchantress, a very powerful kind of witch, who could work magic and enchant things like you wouldn't believe. For my fifth birthday, she offered me a gift – a spell, or enchanted object, that would do whatever I wished. I'd always loved the swans that lived in the river beside our castle, so I asked her to give me a cloak that would allow me to transform into a swan. She made the cloak, and warned me that I might only use it at night, when no one would see me. When I returned the next morning, I was so loathe to turn back into a girl again, that she promised I might go out another night, and the next, until I spent every day as a girl, and every night as a swan.

"Until I grew too big for the cloak, so it no longer covered me. I wept and I raged for days, until my fairy godmother, which is what that witch told me she was, made me a new cloak, bigger and wider, until I outgrew that one, too. Over and over again, until I was a woman grown, and ready to find my mate.

"I met him on the river at dawn, the biggest, handsomest swan you ever saw. He swam close behind me, and nipped at the base of my neck. Before I knew it, he took me, the weight of him sending me so low in the water for a moment, I thought I would sink, before he was done. Three times, he took me, as the sun rose, before I could bring myself to part from him and fly home. The next night, I could scarcely wait for the sun to set before returning to him. He had made me his, pinning me beneath him as he took his pleasure, and I could think of nothing else but him, on me, in me, like nothing I had ever felt before.

"Until one day, my father told me I was betrothed to some king in the mountains, and that I must leave that very day, for the King had arrived to claim me. I begged my fairy godmother to help me, to stop the marriage, for I had fallen in love with a swan, my mate, and together, we hatched a plan. She gave me two potions – one that would turn a swan into a man, and one that would dispatch a man direct. I was to wait until our wedding night, when I was to pour a cup of wine for the King, and mix the poison into the wine so that he might drink it, and die. The other potion I was to mix with one of the King's hairs, before pouring three drops over my mate. My mate would then transform into the King, and together we could dispose of the King's body, before reigning together side by side, as king and queen. I was already carrying my mate's child – twins, actually, though my son did not survive.

"My mate followed us in the air, all the way to the King's castle, biding his time as the celebrations began. For days, the court feasted and danced, while the court tailors made me a gown fit for a queen. I was constantly surrounded by courtiers, never able to don my cloak and see my mate. Finally, the day of the wedding arrived. We said our vows before the priest in the cathedral, amid so much singing, my head ached before we were even halfway through.

"Then came the wedding feast. I sat beside the King and smiled, for I knew my wait was almost over. I would see my mate again, and we could be together.

"Course after course came out. All manner of dishes, more than I could count, until they brought out a platter that was the chef's specialty – roast swan. Only the biggest, plumpest swan would do for the King's wedding feast, and they'd assembled him with all his feathers, he looked so lifelike, though beneath that finery, he'd been roasted well past death.

"I screamed at the sight of him, nearly fell over in a faint, and the King, he just laughed, as if it was a great joke, before pulling my mate's head clean off his butchered corpse, to show me that the bird was dead. As if that could comfort me!

"They carried me to bed, those courtiers who pretended to be my friends, but I would not speak to anyone until my fairy godmother came. I asked her to bring me my vial of poison, so that I might drink it myself and join my mate in death, and she brought me a vial, but all it contained was a sort of sleeping potion that left me helpless on the bed. Then she told me that we must make a new plan. I must allow the King to take me, and be his obedient wife, so that when my mate's child was born, the King would think it his own, and my mate's child would inherit the throne.

"My son did not survive the birth, but my

daughter did. And I vowed when you were born, Odette, that no son of his would survive, so that the throne would be yours when the King was dead. So I birthed child after child for him, but only the girls lived. Now you are a woman grown, nay, a woman mated, just like I was, and I shall give you the choice I never had. You will get to live out your life with your mate, and I shall take the poison I wished for on my wedding night, so the King will never know how to find you!"

At such a story, Swanhild could scarcely think. No wonder the Queen was mad, if this was her tale. So she did not have time to resist before the Queen snatched her up and carried her to the nursery, where eleven other swans milled about, honking in distress. The Queen dropped her in the middle of them, and they flapped and honked, stray feathers flying through the air like fog so Swanhild could not see until it was too late.

A vial tinkled to the ground, shattered into a hundred shards, followed by a thump as the

Queen's body landed atop it, gasping for a breath she could not take, for the poison had stolen it from her. "Fly, Odette," she gasped out before her eyes closed for the final time.

No - no! Swanhild shouted, or at least she tried to, but all she could do was honk, so honk she did, until a servant came running. Her scream alerted everyone else, until finally, the King himself entered the nursery. He took one look at his Queen, then a longer look at the room full of swans, before he shook his head.

"Someone see to the Queen. Someone shut the swans in that room, so they cannot escape. And then find me whoever transformed my daughters into swans and make them change them back or I shall have their head for this!"

It all happened too quickly for Swanhild to form any sort of plan. The Queen was carried out, the door was shut, and she was stuck in a room with eleven panicked swans. Worse, all her worst curses all sounded like either a honk or a hiss.

Twenty-Seven

As Raphael had feared, when they returned to Mirroten, Swanhild was nowhere to be found. He headed straight for Mistress Sara's house, where she insisted he join them for dinner.

After he'd told them Swanhild's tale, he asked, "So, will you help me find her, Mistress Sara?"

"No," Zoticus said, setting down his cup. "Lady Sara's needed here, in case any more of the late Bishop's men try to take Mirroten from her. But I'd intended to pay a visit to King Bela and his court, if only to tell him about the late Bishop, so I'd be happy to help you find your lost bride. In fact, I have just the thing to get us there, too…I found it while I was going through my things. It's been so long since I'd seen it, I'd forgotten about it, which is just as well, seeing as this thing has a habit of toppling cities. Not to mention the Emperor would kill to get his hands on it. Would you believe I found it in a Rialto canal? I think if we arrive at night, so no one sees us, and I put it back into my bag when we arrive, we might be able to risk it."

None of this made sense to Raphael, but he wasn't going to refuse Zoticus's help. When he saw what Zoticus had found in a canal, though, he did wonder if the man had gone mad.

"That's a wooden horse," Raphael said, walking around it, hoping it might look like something more than a worn children's toy if he but looked at it from the right angle, but nothing changed. "I don't see how it will help us."

Zoticus climbed onto the horse. "That's because you've never seen it fly." He touched something on the horse's neck and it rose several feet into the air.

"We're going to fly a wooden horse to court to rescue Swanhild?" Raphael asked. Maybe he was the one who was mad, for even considering this.

"Well, unless you can cast portals like an enchantress, it's the quickest way to reach it. And you did say the King thinks your bride is his daughter, and he wants her to marry some prince…"

Raphael grabbed the horse's tail, and hauled himself up behind Zoticus. "I lost her once. I won't lose her again!"

Zoticus laughed. "Never underestimate a witch, boy, or any woman who truly knows her heart. If she wants to marry you more than some prince, she will stop at nothing until things work out in her favour. You'll see. If we arrive in time..."

The horse whooshed upward so fast, Raphael suspected he'd left his stomach and the rest of his innards on the ground below. But then the creature surged forward so quickly, it stole his breath, too, so it was all he could do to hang on until they reached the King's court.

Twenty-Eight

"Wake up, boy, we're here," Zoticus said.

Raphael blinked blearily up at him. Somehow, he'd fallen asleep on the ground, and the flying wooden horse he'd been dreaming about was nowhere to be seen.

Zoticus grinned and patted the small pouch at his belt. "You'd never know what you can fit inside a magic pouch until you own one, and sometimes, I even surprise myself. Tell yourself you dreamed it all, and it'll be easier. If word reached the Emperor that you knew where to find the enchanted horse, you'd spend the rest of your life in one of his torture chambers, and Mirroten would need to find itself a new apothecary."

Raphael shook his head. One moment, he thought Zoticus was an ordinary man, skilled with weapons and herbs, until he said things like that, and reminded Raphael that the assassin's life was stranger than anything he could imagine. "How are we to get into the King's court?" he asked.

"Well, me, I'll probably just walk in and ask for an audience. King Bela and me go way back. I'm sure he still owes me a favour or two, and then there's the matter of that bishop believing he could claim Lady Sara's lands. You, however, might have a harder time of it. Or you would if the King weren't looking for a man of your talents right now. You see, the whole city is buzzing about the King's latest proclamation. He's looking for a man who can transform a swan into a woman, and from what you've told me, I think you're the man he's looking for. Your job is to persuade him."

Raphael's heart sank. "And what if I can't?"

"Then I believe the King will throw in his dungeon for a few days, along with all the other charlatans, which I imagine he'll release once he meets you."

"Why?"

"Because he's not really looking for a man who can turn a swan into a woman. He's looking for whoever turned his daughters into swans, and when you point at the Queen, I imagine you'll have his attention."

That didn't sound like a good idea, either, but Raphael didn't have anything better, so he forced himself to trudge after Zoticus into the city. The sun had risen by the time they'd trekked all the way up to the castle from the city gates, and the doors to the throne hall were wide open. A crowd of courtiers and common petitioners stood inside, for the only seat was the throne on the dais, where the King sat. A wooden cage rested at his feet with what looked like a swan inside.

"Swanhild!" Raphael blurted out, ready to rush forward to release her, but something caught the back of his tunic and stopped him short.

"That's not your bride, boy," Zoticus said. "It's just an ordinary swan. Nothing magical about it. The King's gone through a dozen birds already, and this one here's lucky number thirteen. Several have been poisoned by charlatans' potions, a couple were burned, one managed to break out of its cage and fly out of the hall, and I don't know what happened to the others. Nothing good, as I understand it. Which is why he's using normal swans to test people, before he lets anyone near his daughters. He's got no sons, you see, so he needs those girls to marry and give him an heir."

Raphael didn't want to think about what the King would do when he found out that his daughters were all dead.

"You go up to talk to the King. I'll speak to

the herald, so he'll announce me when it's my turn. Don't worry, I'll find you when it's time to leave," Zoticus said, strolling through the crowd as if it didn't exist. People just seemed to move to give him a path.

Raphael had to weave through people to approach the dais, the crowd growing thicker, the closer he got.

Two swans met unfortunate ends before Raphael could reach the steps before the throne, and three more corpses were carried away by servants before Raphael could get a close enough look at the swan to see that it didn't have the cloak clasp on its breast that Swanhild had. Zoticus was right – this was an ordinary swan, and not a princess.

Raphael took a deep breath. This was to save Swanhild, he reminded himself. "Your Majesty, you're wasting your time. If you really want to see someone transform a swan into a woman, first you need to find a woman who was transformed into a swan."

The King looked straight at him. "What's

your name, man?"

"Raphael, Master Apothecary of Mirroten," he said proudly.

"Mirroten? The plague town? There's no one left in Mirroten!" someone shouted.

The King waved them into silence. "I ask again. What's your name, man, and where are you from?"

"I am Raphael, Master Apothecary of Mirroten, and anyone who tells you the town is empty is a liar, Your Majesty, for Lady Sara holds those lands still!"

The Kind looked disgruntled. "Yes. Well. Be that as it may, there is the matter of this swan. Master Apothecary, can you turn it into a woman?"

"No, Your Majesty, for it is nothing but an ordinary swan. But if you have a swan who only wears that form because of some spell, who was once a woman, then I may be able to help you."

The King beckoned to one of his guards. "Take him to the dungeons. He knows something. Have him questioned."

Two guards seized Raphael by the arms and started to drag him away before he could protest.

"Master Zoticus," the herald boomed, and everyone, from the King right down to the guards bracketing Raphael, froze.

"Master Zoticus," the King said, as the man himself strode into view. "To what do we owe this honour?"

"I've come to swear fealty. I believe it's customary, when one of your landholders marries, and while the lands are my wife's, I thought it might be nice to come and do a bit of swearing anyway." With that, Zoticus knelt, rattled off the vows, and rose to his feet again.

The King appeared perplexed. "You have a wife?"

Zoticus beamed. "Oh, indeed I do. One of your most loyal landholders – Lady Sara of Mirroten. Why, would you believe the Bishop of Rialto tried to spread a plague across her lands, and take them for himself? Of course, being the virtuous lady she is, God was on her side, not the vile Bishop's, and struck him down for his crimes. Before more than a dozen witnesses, too."

The King did not look pleased. "How fortunate for Lady Sara."

"Oh, no, it's me who is the lucky one! Her people would do anything for her. When she welcomed me into Mirroten, they accepted me as one of their own. In fact, I think I might just retire there with my lovely wife, and maybe raise a family." He smiled. "And how is your family, Bela? Are your daughters well? What about your wife?"

The King rose abruptly. "This audience is over. Master Zoticus, if you will join me…"

The guards remembered themselves, and resumed dragging Raphael out of the hall.

Zoticus snapped his fingers. "You two. Release my apothecary. He may be of service to the King."

The guards let go of Raphael so quickly, he landed on his backside. Before they could seize him again, he was on his feet, dusting himself off, running to catch up with Zoticus and the King.

He reached them just in time to hear the end of the King's tale: "…and she was dead. Dead! All my daughters turned into swans. I could not make any sense of it, and, worse, there is not a single person who witnessed what happened who can explain it to me!" The King shook his head. "I offered untold riches – his own weight in gold, and a princess for a bride, if any man could change them back, but all I get is burned feathers and dead birds and fools! If your apothecary can do something for them, I will double the reward. Give him a place at court. Anything to the man who can give me back my daughters!"

He gestured at the door in front of him. "They're in there. Please, Master Zoticus, if you or your apothecary can help me…I will be forever in your debt. I will give you anything you ask. Lands. Titles. Anything."

Zoticus waved Raphael forward. "You hear

that? The King wants to be indebted to you. That's not the kind of offer you refuse. Especially if you're looking to get married and start a family."

Raphael took a deep breath and pushed open the door.

Twenty-Nine

Swanhild felt like she'd been flying around forever. First to the window, then to the door, but she couldn't open either of them, for the door was bolted from the outside and her wings were not strong enough to push the window shutters open. Yet she had to find a way out, to free the other swans, and fly back to Raphael.

If she could only take her feather cloak off, she could throw open the shutters, but no amount of pecking at the clasp would make it release her from her feathered prison.

She cursed the Queen, whose madness had imprisoned her here, and she cursed the window shutters, for every time she flew at them, feathers tore out of her wings, so that she could almost see her skin where only feathers should be.

No…it looked like human skin, an arm beneath the feathers. What if…

If she could tear the cloak off, instead of unfastening the clasp, would that help her return to her true form? It was worth a shot…

She flew at the window, slamming her body against the shutters again and again until her bones ached and feathers flew everywhere. Too many – she could not stay aloft on what was left, and she plummeted to the ground, landing on top of several other swans. The birds squawked and flapped, attacking her and each other in their panic.

Beneath their onslaught, something tore, and she saw her hand, then an arm. Swanhild threw herself at another group of birds, sending the whole room into a frenzy. Beaks tore at her, wings beat her, and Swanhild staggered to the window, hand outstretched. The shutter…if she could only unfasten the shutters…

But while one hand appeared human, she was still only the height of a bird. This would not do. She scrabbled at the clasp with her fingers, tearing the fabric in her haste to break free. The shredded cloak fell to the flagstones, a mess of ribbons with only a few feathers left and a hole where the clasp had once been.

With both hands now, Swanhild reached for the shutters, and threw them open wide. Then she seized a swan and tossed it out the window. Then another, and another, until all eleven of them had formed up into a sort of flock, waiting for her to join them.

Her heart twinged in her chest. With her feather cloak in ribbons and her mother dead, Swanhild would never be able to transform into a swan again. Never soar through the skies, drift across a lake, ride the updrafts into the clouds…

But the other swans would, as was right, and they would all be free. Free of the mad Queen and this prison of lies.

If only she could unbar the door holding her here, so that she might return home to Raphael. Ugh, she'd settle for someone cleaning up all the feathers. It was enough to make anyone sneeze.

Behind her, the door swung silently open.

Thirty

The door opened, but all Raphael could see was a storm of feathers, flying in all directions. Then the cloud cleared, and standing in the middle of the room was…

"Swanhild?"

She didn't seem to hear him at first, for she was facing the window, but the third time he said her name, she turned around. "Raphael?"

"What in heaven's name is going on here? Who are you and where are my daughters?"

the King demanded.

Swanhild winced, then dropped a curtsy, as prettily as any courtier. "Your Majesty, I am Swanhild of Mirroten. Perhaps I can shed some light on the matter." She ducked her head. "First, my condolences on the loss of your Queen. She was quite driven mad with grief, I believe, when the plague killed her daughters."

"But…the swans…" the King blurted out.

"The swans you saw in here were not your daughters, but birds that had been bespelled to look like your daughters. When the Queen died, the spell wore off, and they were trapped in here, until I released them. The poor birds were quite frantic. If they were stuck in here much longer, they might have hurt themselves."

"So where are my children?"

"I believe if you sent someone to your hunting lodge on the lake near Mirroten, you will find where they are buried. They died of the plague, Your Majesty, for which there is no cure. I am a herbalist, and my betrothed is an apothecary, and while we do all we can, we cannot cure the plague." She bowed her head. "I am so sorry for your loss."

"But…but…my children…"

Zoticus stepped up to the King's shoulder. "Bela, I think this is where you command your servants to bring you a cask of your strongest wine, and together we drink to the memory of your wife and children. I've pieced together much of this tale already, but you deserve to hear it all. And these two should go home to Mirroten, where they have a wedding to celebrate and probably plenty of herbs to prepare before the winter. In fact, that vile Bishop of Rialto was responsible for your daughters' deaths, even as he tried to rob my wife. Would you like to hear how he died?"

Zoticus threw an arm around the King's shoulder as he began his tale, shooing Raphael and Swanhild away.

Raphael looked at Swanhild, who shrugged.

"So, we go home?" she asked.

"If the King lets us leave, yes."

"And what then? We just settle down in Mirroten, and live our lives again? After all that has happened?"

Raphael wrapped his arm around Swanhild's shoulder. "First, we get married. Then, we spend at least a week in bed together. Maybe even two. Then, we start our new lives together. And, after all that's happened to us, I mean to spend the rest of my life making you happy. I made a promise to your mother."

"Did she threaten you with the devil, or her ghost?"

"She didn't have to. I love you more than the moon and all the stars in the sky. I love every part of you, inside and out. You are my only love, because I love no one else, and I never will. I mean to make love to you every morning, and every night, and spend every hour between making you happy. If you'll still have me, Swanhild."

"Yes. A thousand times yes."

About the Author

Demelza Carlton has always loved the ocean, but on her first snorkelling trip she found she was afraid of fish.

She has since swum with sea lions, sharks and sea cucumbers and stood on spray drenched cliffs over a seething sea as a seven-metre cyclonic swell surged in, shattering a shipwreck below.

Demelza now lives in Perth, Western Australia, the shark attack capital of the world.

The *Ocean's Gift* series was her first foray into fiction, followed by her suspense thriller *Nightmares* trilogy. She swears the *Mel Goes to Hell* series ambushed her on a crowded train and wouldn't leave her alone.

Want to know more? You can follow Demelza on Facebook, Twitter, YouTube or her website, Demelza Carlton's Place at:

www.demelzacarlton.com

More Books by Demelza Carlton

<u>Colony: Holiday series</u>
Cowboys and Aliens (#1)
Ghost (#2)
Vulcan (#3)
Cupid (#4)
Valentine(#5)
Prometheus (#6)

Colony: Nyx series

Fang (#1)

Talon (#2)

Claw (#3)

<u>**Siren of Secrets series**</u>

Ocean's Secret (#1)

Ocean's Gift (#2)

Ocean's Infiltrator (#3)

<u>Nightmares Trilogy</u>

Nightmares of Caitlin Lockyer (#1)

Necessary Evil of Nathan Miller (#2)

Afterlife of Alana Miller (#3)

<u>**Romance Island Resort series**</u>

Maid for the Rock Star (#1)

The Rock Star's Email Order Bride (#2)

The Rock Star's Virginity (#3)

The Rock Star and the Billionaire (#4)

The Rock Star Wants A Wife (#5)

The Rock Star's Wedding (#6)

Maid for the South Pole (#7)

<u>**Romance a Medieval Fairytale series**</u>

Enchant: Beauty and the Beast Retold

Dance: Cinderella Retold

Fly: Goose Girl Retold

Revel: Twelve Dancing Princesses
Retold

Silence: Little Mermaid Retold

Awaken: Sleeping Beauty Retold

Embellish: Brave Little Tailor Retold

Appease: Princess and the Pea Retold

Blow: Three Little Pigs Retold

Return: Hansel and Gretel Retold

Wish: Aladdin Retold

Melt: Snow Queen Retold

Spin: Rumpelstiltskin Retold

Kiss: Frog Prince Retold

Reflect: Snow White Retold

Roar: Goldilocks Retold

Cobble: Elves and the Shoemaker Retold

Float: Enchanted Horse Retold

Steal: Forty Thieves Retold

Call: Pied Piper Retold

Fall: Scheherazade Retold
Feather: Swan Maidens Retold
Cross: Billy Goats Gruff Retold
Weave: Rapunzel Retold
Claim: Puss in Boots Retold
Curse: Rose Red Retold
Cross: Three Billy Goats Gruff Retold
Weave: Rapunzel Retold
Claim: Puss in Boots Retold

<u>**Heart of Stone series**</u>

Heart of Steel (#0)

Broken Chains (#1)

Broken Bonds (#2)

Broken Dreams (#3)

<u>**Heart of Steel series**</u>

Heart of Steel (#0)

Stone Guardian (#1)

Stone Champion (#2)

Stone Sentinel (#3)

Stone Shadow (#4)